Rabbit's Foot

Rabbit's Foot

A Gift from My Father

Allan Horlick

RABBIT'S FOOT COMMUNICATIONS, INC.
Washington DC

Rabbit's Foot
by Allan Horlick

Published by: Rabbit's Foot Communications, Inc.

www.rabbitsfootbook.com

ISBN - Hard Cover: 978-0-9832603-0-1
ISBN - Soft Cover: 978-0-9832603-1-8
ISBN - eBook: 978-0-9832603-2-5
Library of Congress Control Number: 2011922741

First Edition. Printed in the United States of America
18 17 16 15 14 13 12 11 1 2 3 4 5

"Bear Down, Chicago Bears" was written by Al Hoffman (writing as Jerry Downs), circa 1941

To Nathan Jewel Horlick—my father.
He loved helping people, and he loved to see them smile.

Prologue

March 13, 1945
Caraballo Mountains, Luzon, Philippines

T he rabbit's foot swung from the back pocket of
Bob's fatigues like a furry little tail. Bob didn't
care how stupid it looked. He was the luckiest man
alive, and he wasn't ashamed to show it.

Like his best friend, Al, slogging up the jungle trail
behind him, he was only twenty-five, but three years of
hard fighting across the Pacific had made them both
battle-savvy warriors. Pearl Harbor seemed like a hundred
years ago.

A month earlier, they had been transferred to a new
division to join the 33rd Infantry when it sailed into
Lingayen Gulf. Bob thought back to that first morning
when a Jeep dropped them off pier-side, and they watched
their new comrades come shuffling down the gangplanks.

They all marched to a nearby staging area for an early-
morning briefing. Even at 7 o'clock, the thick, damp air gave
the newbies their first hint of what was in store for them.
The major—short, stocky, and already sweating through
his bulging uniform—sounded like the accountant he'd
been before the war as he told the troops they would only
be doing a little "mopping up."

Bob remembered the major's exact words: "This war is
won. The whole damn world knows it. You men just do

what remains to be done. Then you can sail home to your wives or girlfriends and get that big hero's welcome you've been dreaming about."

Bob had looked around at all of the fresh young faces nodding in agreement and thought for a moment that he was the only one who wasn't buying it—until Al hissed, "Do you believe this crap?"

Then the major wrapped it up: "Look sharp out there, men. Do what you've been trained to do, and let's get the hell out of here."

Like the major said, everyone knew the war was won. How could you not? The problem was, nobody had told the surviving Japanese soldiers—soldiers who had taken a pledge of honor to fight to the death.

Unlike Bob and Al, most of the Illinois boys in the 33rd hadn't seen much combat: the Prairie Division, fresh from training in Hawaii and pretty green. Green enough to believe the major when he called what they were in for "mopping up."

The sharp crack of a rifle brought Bob's mind back to the moment.

"Sniper!" Al shouted.

Instinctively, Bob and the others fell to the ground, taking cover in the thick jungle underbrush. Bob tried to block out the image of the corporal on the point who'd taken the sniper's bullet and silently crumbled to the ground. He wondered, where's the major now? "Mopping up."

There was silence for a moment. A few of the seven remaining members of the patrol tried to peek out in search of the enemy ahead.

"Grenade," someone yelled as the deadly orb flew over their heads. It landed with a dull thud twenty feet away, and a moment later a deafening blast erupted, killing the two soldiers behind them and ripping open a third.

A Japanese battle cry from the brush triggered a cross fire that pinned the GIs to the ground. Driven by terror, two greenies up front broke and started running back down the path. Watching in horror, Bob knew those boys didn't have a chance. They both fell, one dead, the other dying, only a few feet from where Bob and Al, now the only two remaining survivors, had taken cover.

The old friends shared a silent, knowing stare. They'd been here before and didn't need words to communicate.

Al, being in front, quickly stood and sprayed the woods with fire. Bob instinctively reached back to rub his rabbit's foot for good luck before lunging five feet down the path. And so it went: each friend took a turn putting up covering fire while the other retreated down the hill. The plan was to leapfrog like this for as long as they could, praying that either the Japs showed themselves or the cavalry came riding in.

On the third rotation down the mountainside, another grenade exploded to their right just as Al stood to fire. Shrapnel tore at the side of his face, barely missing Bob, who was already scampering forward. Bob glanced back to see if Al had escaped the blast. Instead he saw that the explosion had spun his wounded friend around, causing his rifle to recoil.

Instinctively, Bob tried to turn away, just as he felt the searing pain of Al's stray bullet piercing his flesh. And in that moment, Al too realized he'd shot his best friend.

3

Nearly blinded by the blood streaming into his eyes, his head pounding from the ringing in his ears, Al followed his instincts and began running away from the gunfire. But only for a few feet before his foot caught on something, sending him sprawling to the ground. Totally disoriented, Al struggled to his knees to make one more attempt at escape. Rising, pain throbbing from his bloody face, he thought he could hear the Japanese barking orders. They were getting closer.

And he wanted to run, but he couldn't. He couldn't run, because he knew that what caused him to trip wasn't a jungle root or a dead animal. It was Bob.

Frozen for just a moment, he willed himself to turn and run back up the hill. Back toward the attacking Japs. Back to his friend lying on the ground, bleeding from the gunshot that he himself had fired.

He found Bob right where he knew he would be, lying face-down among the undergrowth. Al grabbed him by his shoulder and rolled him on his side as bullets began to fly all around them.

Kneeling at his side, Al cradled Bob's head and saw his eyelids begin to flutter. Their faces only inches apart, Al whispered between teeth clenched in pain. "Looks like your rabbit's foot may be losing its power, buddy."

Before Bob could answer, Al stole a glance up at the slowly advancing Japs—bayonets fixed and now less than one hundred feet away. Silently, he checked his rifle, only to find that the action was jammed. Bob's weapon was nowhere to be found. Al was thankful for the dense jungle cover, but he knew it was only a matter of time.

Bob's eyes flickered open. Not seeming to notice the

bloody pulp of Al's cheek, he simply asked, "Can I see it? Can you give me my rabbit's foot?"

Al took another look back and motioned for his friend to whisper. Then he reached behind Bob and, with a single, firm yank, tore the rabbit's foot away from the fatigues. Gently he handed it over.

In the dim light of the overgrowth, Bob tried to make it out. He studied his rabbit's foot as if he'd never seen it before.

"What the hell, you moron! Look at this. You shot it! You shot my lucky rabbit's foot."

Al took it back, and sure enough, the metal clasp at the top was badly burned and dented from his stray bullet.

"Okay, let me get this straight," he whispered. "I come running back up the hill to save your ass. Now we're both about to get killed, and you're pissed off that I shot your stupid trinket?"

Bullets started flying again. A quick glance up showed the nearest Japanese soldier standing still, less than forty feet away.

Snatching his rabbit's foot back, Bob propped himself up on one elbow. "Yeah, I'm pissed. Not only did you shoot my rabbit's foot, you shot me in the ass too!"

The ground rumbled as more soldiers made a charge from behind them. Shooting. Yelling out commands. Flinging grenades. The two friends realized at the same moment that they were saved: a full platoon of Illinois boys from the 33rd came charging up the hill, forcing the enemy into retreat.

Bob managed a smirk: "Who says the luck wore off my rabbit's foot?"

"Medic!" Al shouted as the 33rd drew nearer.

As the medic dropped down on one knee to tend the wounded soldiers, he stared in disbelief at two bleeding Yanks arguing with each other like an old married couple.

Al waved the medic away from his bloody face, signaling that he should treat Bob first.

"So you're not even going to thank me for coming back for you?"

Bob only shrugged. "Why would I thank you? I knew you'd come back."

———

Three months later, on June 15, 1945, the two soldiers were recuperating in the cramped sick bay of a troop carrier bound for Hawaii. The same day in Chicago, a young colored boy in the upper deck of Comiskey Park squirmed in anticipation as he waited for the thirteenth annual National Negro League All-Star Game to begin.

It was a mild day, and pretty much every seat in the stadium was filled. The previous year, the game had nearly been cancelled due to a players' strike, but that had been settled when the players each got a $90 pay raise. This year, though, there was never a doubt that the game would be played, and the crowd buzzed with excitement. But no one was more excited to be there than the boy high above left field. He was wearing his favorite red plaid shirt along with his most prized possession: the baseball mitt his father had given him last Christmas.

Today was going to be his special day. With four younger brothers and sisters, he rarely got his parents to himself. Worst of all, he didn't get to see much of his dad, who worked every shift he could get as a bus driver for the Chicago Transit Authority. But not this afternoon. This afternoon was his.

But where was his dad?

Father and son had been planning this outing for weeks, and so far everything was perfect. His dad was to meet him at the stadium as soon as he got off work. Aunt Maxine had walked him over to the ballpark and given him his ticket as he got into line. She'd also given him 50 cents for snacks as her own special gift, which meant he had almost a dollar in his pocket, even after he'd bought a bottle of Coca-Cola. An usher had helped him find his seat. Now, he was taking it all in: the aroma of hot dogs and popcorn, the slow, steady wave of people trudging up the stairs, but most of all the sea of green that filled the vista from the concrete entrance ramp to his section high above left field. He watched intently as the batting practice, the introductions from around home plate, and the national anthem all came and went. But no dad.

A pretty woman smiled kindly at him as she and the man with her slid by to take their seats next to him. It didn't take her long to start up a conversation.

"Which team are you for, honey?"

She had the nicest smile he had ever seen and looked so beautiful in her flowered dress with a huge belt that matched the light brown bonnet on her head. He wanted to impress her with his knowledge.

"I'm for the West. I want to see Jackie Robinson running those bases. My dad says he's the best there is."

The woman nodded her head. "Sounds like you're quite a fan. Did you come here all by yourself to see Mr. Jackie Robinson?"

The boy fibbed just a little. "Yep, I walked over here all by myself. But I'm meeting my dad here as soon as he gets off of work."

She didn't respond, but she did seem a little relieved. She smiled once more and turned back to her companion.

In the third inning, he bought a hot dog from one of the vendors, and a few minutes later, another Coke to wash it down. He tried to act like he wasn't scared, but his constant looks over to the entrance gave him away.

"You okay, sweetie?"

"Yes, ma'am. I'm fine. The West is up by two."

"Your dad's probably just late getting off work."

"Yes, ma'am."

By the seventh inning, the West's lead had grown to three, but he wasn't paying much attention. Mostly, he just stared straight out at the field.

The nice woman put her hand on his arm. "What's your name?"

He couldn't bring himself to look at her as he mumbled, "James Artis."

"Well, James Artis, is there anyone you'd like me to call? There's a pay phone back by those concessions."

By the eighth inning she'd persuaded him to write his phone number on her program book, and she told her friend she'd be right back. When she returned, she whispered something to the man next to her, and he snapped his head around.

James couldn't hear exactly what he said, but he sure

seemed angry as he gestured wildly to the action on the field. The woman just leaned into him and once again whispered in his ear.

She turned back to James and smiled sweetly as she took his hand. But there were tears running down her cheeks.

"Come on, baby. We're going to walk you home."

1

Sarah's Funeral

Thinking about the weather isn't usually considered strange. Still, here I am sitting at my own wife's funeral and, sonofabitch, would you believe I'm thinking about the weather.

It seems like only from a distance that I hear the words of those who stand by Sarah's coffin to speak. I can hear crying, too, especially the pitiful tiny sobs of the small children I love, but none of that is in my mind right now. Just the weather.

It's the sunlight that's throwing me off. Funerals are meant to be held on dark, rainy days. But here I am, sitting in the chapel, and all I can see is the brilliant Maryland winter sunlight *gushing* through the stained-glass windows and shining a spotlight on Sarah's coffin.

Where are the dark clouds? Where is the rain? I mean, somebody has died here, for God's sake, and I'd be a lot more comfortable with the whole thing if it was raining. Jeez.

Indiana. Now there's a place that knows about rain. Rain like it rained that day so many years ago when we buried my father. I was only ten years old, but I can still remember that cold winter rain like it was yesterday. Then again, maybe that's because I've thought about it every day since.

I can still see my childhood home in Hammond filled with all the family and friends who had come back with us from the cemetery. I can still smell the tuna noodle casserole some of the neighbor ladies brought over, and to this day I still can't eat the stuff. Like snapshots burned in my mind, I see their sad faces as one by one they took turns telling me how much they loved my father or how proud of me he was or—my personal favorite—that now I was the man of the house. Sure, I was only ten years old, but for my mother's sake, they said I needed to be a man. And then, of course, they would all hit me with the big one: "Your father was such a great man."

Sometimes they would say it with a hand on my shoulder, or maybe whisper it in my ear through a crushing hug. Maybe they would be crying, or maybe they'd be smiling sadly. It didn't matter, because they would all say the same thing: how much they loved him and what a great man he was.

Well, a lot of good their love was doing him now, right? And they could cry all they wanted to, but not me. No tears from me. Not one. If he was so great, why did he have to get himself killed?

I had run out of the house and away from all those people. No jacket. No hat. Just me in the freezing January rain. Oh, and one more thing. I also had that stupid rabbit's foot key chain that my father had given me only a few days before. It was supposed to be a lucky charm. Yeah, right. My dad would have told you that I wouldn't have even been born if it weren't for that thing, but to me, well, now it all just seemed like a big lie.

So there I was, a ten-year-old man, standing on the curb in the cold, blowy Indiana rain, looking down at my soaking feet, now almost ankle-deep in a miniature river racing down to the drain a few feet away. Thrusting my freezing hands deep down into my pockets I felt it, soft and fluffy on the outside, hard bone on the inside, and I knew right then what I was going to do.

I yanked it out of my pocket and threw it into the little river at my feet. Then I stood there, watching with grim satisfaction as the water carried it away toward the drain, slowly at first and then faster. But then, as if to mock me, it just floated there, right over the steel slats of the street drain, just bobbing up and down, caught somehow, I suppose. It seemed to ask me, "Are you sure, Josh? Are you really sure?" But I just stood there in the rain, not wanting a second chance, just watching, watching, watching, and then in a flash, it's gone.

Down the drain. Into the dark. See you later, Dad.

———————

So what the hell kind of funeral is this? No rain, hardly even a cloud. Sure, it's winter, but with the sun and the brilliant blue Maryland sky, it might as well be August.

And there's that weeping again. And somebody else is standing up, speaking words that sound so familiar. Words about Sarah being a great person, words about how much people loved her.

Sarah, Sarah, Sarah.

I wish you and my father had met.

2

January 28, 1983
Ninety-Four Hours before Sarah's Death

S arah! Get the door. Sarah!"

"You don't have to shout. I'm right here," Sarah snaps. She is holding our little three-year-old, Sophie and her brand new Cabbage Patch doll, gently bouncing her up and down in one arm to try to stop her crying, while towing six-year-old Richie with her other hand. Pretty amazing how she can be gently coo-cooing one of the kids at exactly the same time that she is totally unloading on me. Kind of like a great NFL quarterback who can look left and throw right in a single move.

"I'd be happy to get the door."

Oh boy, here it comes.

"I'll get the door, and why don't you just get Richie dressed, hug Sophie until she stops crying, and then make a list for Sherry of everything she needs to do with the kids this weekend, and get her the phone number of the hotel. After that you can check the freezer for—"

"Fine. I'm going."

Perfect. I'm not up even an hour and I get my first blast. Now I'm headed downstairs to open the door for her sister so that she can rip into me too. Swell.

Rabbit's Foot

I'm only thirty-six years old, and we're living in a beautiful home in Potomac. Nice cars, a club membership, no debts to speak of, and she thinks it just happens by magic. She could take her sweet time packing last night; I had work to do. I didn't get to be the youngest officer and a top attorney in my company by working 9:00 to 5:00. I mean, the whole company is under tremendous pressure to grow our position, and it was my job to finish up a critical strategy report so Grand National wouldn't be on the hook for millions in new claims based on some wacky, experimental x-ray gizmo. Level Three intervention . . . give me a break! Sounds like something the Dolphins might try to throw at the Skins!

OK, deep breath. Just open the door, smile, and say, "Good morning, Sherry. Thanks again for watching the kids this weekend."

God, how I hate that smirk of hers. "Well, look at you, Josh. Nice legs. And I just love how your new burgundy T-shirt goes with those gold boxers."

Washington Redskins
1983
NFC Champions

"Are those your traveling clothes, or do you have some Redskins pants you can throw on, too?"

Okay now, be sweet, pleasant. Don't lose that smile. Don't let her see you blink. "Gee, Sherry, I'd love to stand here and chat with you for a while, but I have to finish packing." Smooth, very smooth. "I was burning the old midnight oil last night."

"In other words, seeing how many claims you could get denied. Important stuff. I talked to Sarah last night, so I know all about your evening. A pity you couldn't make time to say goodnight to the kids."

Just keep smiling.

"Or maybe help out Sarah a little? You do know she had another bad one last night, don't you?"

"Of course I know she had a *bad one*. She has had a bad one every day for the last three months. But she's been to half the doctors in Washington, and nobody can find anything wrong with her. What else can I do?"

"So you're saying it's all in her head, right? You think Sarah isn't in pain?"

Ah, the phone. Saved by the bell. I yell at the staircase, "Good news, honey, Sherry is here, and she is coming up to help you. I'll get the phone. Probably my mom anyway."

Mom is no doubt calling to tell us to have a good time and, of course, to make sure I remember. Like I haven't thought about it every day for more than twenty-five years now, and even more so when Super Bowl weekend rolls around. This *should* be the best week of the year for me. Especially this year, with my Skins going up against the Dolphins. But there it is, another year's gone by without him, and Mom thinks she has to remind me.

Back in 1956 they didn't have Super Bowls. But my dad said it was going to be the best weekend of his life: December 30, 1956, to be exact, when his beloved Chicago Bears would take on the New York Giants for the NFL Championship. We were going to watch the game together, he promised. But then, surprise, surprise: the game went on, and the Giants killed the Bears. Too bad my dad wasn't alive to see it. He'd gotten himself killed too just three days before.

"Hi, honey. It's Mom." Yeah, surprise, surprise.

"I just called to see how the kids are and to wish you and Sarah a nice time on your trip. Are you excited?"

"The kids are both fine, and you bet I'm excited. You know how much the Redskins mean to me. Watching the game on a large screen with hundreds of fans will be great. How about you, Mom? Any plans for the weekend?"

"You know how I feel about Super Bowl weekend. It seems like every time I turn on the television, all I see is people talking about 'the big game.' Well, it's not the big game to me. It's just a flood of sad memories. You remember what the end of the football season really means to me, don't you? I mean, other than your big football game?"

"Yes, of course I remember." I think she's crying now.

"I know. I still can't believe he's gone either. Twenty-six years now. So sad."

I've gotta get her off this before I go nuts. "Have you seen any of your old friends lately?"

"Well, I bumped into Roberta Johnson last week."

Oh shit. I had to ask.

"She said that Sammy always asks about you. You know, he lives in the D.C. area too, and you're both lawyers, so you really ought to give him a call sometime. You two were such good friends growing up."

"Mom, the last time I spoke to Sammy was at our ten-year high school reunion, and that was just a quick hello when he tracked me down at the bar."

"Well, Mrs. Johnson is very proud of him."

"That's nice for Mrs. Johnson. Personally, I don't think that he has two nickels to rub together. Listen, Mom, I really would like to talk to you some more, but I've gotta run. I still haven't finished packing, and our flight leaves in a few hours. Okay?"

It's just about an exact replay of the conversation we have every year on Super Bowl weekend, except this time I get to cut it short so that I can pack.

I think the whole vacation thing threw her for a loop, especially when I told her the trip was free. A Premier VIP guest of the casino on Paradise Island: room, food, drinks, even the airfare! Eat, drink, and be merry, soaking up the sun during the day, then watching the Super Bowl with hundreds of other Redskins (and Dolphins) fans. The only thing is, the rest of those fans are high rollers in the casino, and I'm chump change. They won't get enough action out of me to cover the free drinks at the pool, but there it was, a letter last month inviting me and *my* guest to be guests of the casino. Nice letter to get, wouldn't you say? Somebody's head is going to roll when the pit boss sees me putting only an orange five-dollar chip on the line at the crap table. But that's not my problem.

"Mom, really, I gotta go. Yeah, I love you too. Yeah, you bet. Dad was a great man. One of the best. Okay, gotta go."

I've got to finish packing, which means I can close the door and not listen to Sherry telling Sarah what a jerk I am. I think Sherry hates me simply because of my job. She actually thinks my work hurts more people than it helps! Just because it's my job to figure out how to control our exposure. And guess what? No apologies. I'm good at it! The thing that Sherry, and maybe even my own wife, doesn't understand is that the first obligation of any business is to itself. I know it sounds heartless, Sherry would even say evil, but if a company doesn't take care of itself first, then there is no company. No company means no employees. No employees means no job. No house, cars, or clubs, and no future for Richie and Sophie.

I can't even make it upstairs to finish my packing before the phone starts ringing again.

"Look, Mom, I really can't talk now."

"Er, Mr. Brown? Is this Mr. Josh Brown, director of policyholder relations for the Grand National Insurance Company?"

"Yes, it is. How can I help you?" Might as well be pleasant; this has got to be a friend of my boss's if he has my home number.

"Mr. Brown, my name is Anthony Scappelli. You don't know me, but I have health coverage with your company through my union. The thing is, I'm in a pretty desperate way, and I really appreciate your taking my call."

Swell. Just what I need right now. I have minutes left to pack and get Sarah out the door, and somebody from the office thinks this is a great time for a joke.

"Listen, Mr. Scallini, I'm sure whoever put you up to this little prank has a great sense of humor, but I don't, not when I have to catch a plane, so have a nice day."

"It's Scappelli, Mr. Brown. Anthony Scappelli. I was told to call you because my little daughter is dying and your company won't do anything about it. That sound like a joke to you?"

"Can I ask how you got my home number?"

"Sure. I got a phone call a few minutes ago from a man

who had just reviewed our file. He said I needed to talk to you, that you were the only one who could approve my daughter getting a new procedure so they can operate, and he gave me this number. First nice person I've talked to at Grand National. But he didn't tell me it was your home number, so I'm sorry about that. I'll call your office Monday morning if you like, but I'm begging you, *please,* look at my daughter's file as soon as you can. My baby is dying."

"Mr. Scappelli. I'm sorry for you, I really am. But there's been a mistake here. We have more than a half-million policyholders, and I don't speak to any of them, ever. I'm the director of policyholder relations, Mr. Scappelli, not one of the designated adjustment clerks. I'm sorry about your daughter, but I can't help you. Just call our Claims Department on Monday, and I'm sure someone will be happy to speak with you. Now I have to run. Good luck, Mr. Scappelli."

Having kids of my own, I really do feel sorry for the poor guy, but what am I supposed to do about it? So I hang up and call Philip Townsend. Imagine that, 7:30 in the morning and I'm calling the boss. I'll score some points, too, when I let him know that the new x-ray is dead on delivery. Coffin nailed. We shouldn't have to pay out a penny, so crisis averted, and we live to fight again another day.

"Phil, I told you I'd have it done before my trip. Solid too. It will be years before Level Three isn't considered experimental. I mean give me a break: they're talking about getting images from any angle, even at the core of the brain, and using these images to guide surgery. But our docs will testify that either the patient's brain will be fried, or even if they get some images, the unlucky patient will still hemorrhage and die on the table anyway."

Phil grunts in approval.

"I don't have to tell you, boss, but we can't afford to pay a single claim here, or we will just wind up encouraging these guys. Our engineering consultants from Baker laid it out as plain as day: huge doughnut-shaped machines that patients would actually be rolled into while magnets and God only knows what else go spinning all around them! A handful of tech companies are already spending millions to develop these contraptions, and I'm sure they see big dollars coming back to them from massive patient fees and enormous insurance claims. Level Three my ass. Not on our nickel!"

I catch a glimpse of myself in our hall mirror. I'm grinning from ear to ear.

"Problem solved, Phil. The report is sitting on your private fax machine. I sent it over around 1:00 a.m."

Phil isn't one to mince words. "You're on a rocket, Josh. You've got lightning bolts coming out of your ass, and you've got VP written all over you! Listen, I've gotta run myself, but have a great time in the Bahamas. GO SKINS! And if I ever find out who gave out your home number, he is gone. We take care of our own at Grand National."

"Thanks, boss."

3

December 15, 1956
Twelve Days before My Father Dies

D ad, come on. I'm starving. You promised!"

"You'll make it, Josh. Five more minutes, buddy. Go get your hat and coat. Gloves too."

I've never really minded waiting for my dad. For one thing, I'm used to it. When you own your own business, like my mom and dad do, there are always things to do. Like Mom always tells Dad, a business like Lucky Auto Car Center doesn't run itself.

My dad, Bob—never Robert—Brown started Lucky Auto in 1946 with a VA loan. Before the war he had been a district manager for a large automotive accessory chain in Chicago, but he figured if he could survive being shot in the war, he could make a living running his own business. Hence the name—*Lucky Auto.*

So after the war he left Chicago, looking for virgin territory, and wound up about forty minutes south of Soldier Field in Hammond, Indiana. I think my dad also knew that he could count on my mom, Susan, to do the serious work of actually running the place, freeing him up to do what he did best: entertaining our biggest customers and generally being about the most popular man in Hammond.

23

Last week my dad took me to a pancake breakfast for the Lions Club, which he's been president of for years. With a hundred conversations going on at once, the school gym was so noisy we had to shout to be heard, but when Dad went up on the little stage to thank everyone for coming, the whole room got quiet. Everyone in the gym looked up at him, smiling and waiting for the first of his jokes, or maybe a story.

My mom and dad were college sweethearts. When the war broke out and Dad enlisted, he and my mom ran off and eloped. I guess Mom's family didn't think marriage was such a great idea since she could wind up a widow a few months later, but that didn't stop either of them. Dad never had any doubt he would return. He always considered himself the luckiest man alive, and no amount of combat would change that. My mom and dad were a good team to own a business: she did the work, and he kept the customers happy.

Today is Saturday, the best day of the week for any ten-year-old boy, but especially for me. Every Saturday my mom and dad bring me to work with them, and I love hanging out at the store. Plus, I'm an only child, so what else can they do with me? Of course, when I say I'm an only child, I'm not including James Artis, the young colored man who manages Lucky Auto. Dad says he loves him like a son. That doesn't always go over so well in Hammond, Indiana, where most people don't think like that.

My dad and James go way back. When James was a boy, he was the sole support of his family, and my father gave him his first part-time job. Dad watched James grow into a "fine young man" who put himself through college in the evenings. After college, he entered officers' candidate school during the Korean War, becoming one of the first colored officers to lead integrated troops into battle. When James returned from Korea, my dad hired him as the manager of Lucky Auto, figuring if he could order a bunch of white guys to go over a hill shooting guns, he could probably get them to come to work on time. Sometimes my dad even calls James "Lieutenant," which is pretty funny since my dad never made it past corporal. Dad still loves telling anyone and everyone that James graduated third out of 1,200 in officers' training.

But, like I said, I love coming to the store, and my folks even pay me a little for helping out, but that isn't the best part either. The best part is that every Saturday at lunchtime, my dad and I take off. Dad tells James and my mom not to burn the place down while we're away "planning strategy." Just the two of us. All the guys in the back always yell out, "Have a good one, boss," and my dad gives them a wave over his shoulder. So do I.

Sometimes our "lunch" turns out to be a surprise, like seeing the White Sox play on a sunny Saturday afternoon. One time we made it to Comiskey Park in twenty-seven minutes flat. Or, in the spring, our "lunch" might be fishing at one of the local lakes. Sometimes, my dad secretly packs a little bag with my pajamas and toothbrush, and we head up to northern Michigan for some real fishing.

Most of the time, though, we just go across the street to Giovanni's for lunch, where my dad loves to joke around with the regulars and meet up with his best friend, Al Kaplan, who always sits down with us at our booth. Al is a Hammond policeman, and the first thing I always notice about him is the huge gun on his hip. That and the pink scar on his cheek, where some shrapnel hit him just before he shot my dad in the ass.

"Good morning, Josh. I see you're still dragging the same goofy guy around." I smile back at him and settle in along with all of the other customers in Giovanni's, watching as my dad and Al go through the same greeting ritual they've been doing for years.

Al stares right into my dad's eyes and says, "Hello, Robert," just to piss him off, since he knows better than anyone that my dad hates being called anything but Bob. Then my dad stares right back at Al and says, "Hey there, Eagle Eye. How's your aim today?" Then Dad reaches behind him and pulls out his lucky rabbit's foot charm, which is normally dangling out of his back pocket like a miniature tail. With a flourish, leaning in and eyeball-to-eyeball with the big cop across from him, Dad always sets the rabbit's foot on the table right in front of Al. With this little move anyone watching breaks out laughing and lunch can begin. Any newcomer would probably be totally confused by now and ask what in the world was so funny.

Even during the war my dad kept his lucky rabbit's foot hanging from his back pocket, and when Al shot him, the metal ring at the top of the charm partially deflected the bullet. Or, as my dad would say, it literally saved his balls from being blown off. The rabbit's foot is clearly burned and dented up top, so maybe it's true. My dad and Al both earned Purple Hearts that day, and my dad walked away with a lifelong punch line: "Where was I shot during the war? Right in the ass!"

With the regular little ritual out of the way, the owner, Tony Imperial, motions for our waitress to come over and take our order. I guess I have Ruth to thank for giving me my first real appreciation of breasts. Big, beautiful breasts that my dad said could make it all the way to the Illinois line. It's pretty obvious, even to a ten-year-old, that Ruth, whose best years are probably behind her, loves the attention. She always wears the same white-and-pink uniform with the top two buttons undone, lest there be any doubt that hers are the genuine article. Her blond hair is piled on top of her head and held in place by a red ribbon tied in a perfect bow. She's also wearing the perfume from Marshall Fields that my dad and Al give her every Christmas.

As usual I maneuver to sit on the outside end of the booth, so that when she comes back with our food, she'll bend down right in front of me. Oh man!

As always, Ruth gives Al and me a nice smile but saves the best for Dad. "I see you have your partner with you today."

My dad pretends to push me out of the booth, claiming, "I've never seen this kid before, honest! I have no clue who he is. But I've got an idea. How about if you and me and your beautiful breasts get into my car and drive off into the sunset?"

Ruth smacks my dad across the head with her order pad, and Tony howls from behind the counter. Al rolls his eyes as I turn beet red. This happens every time, but I just can't help it. My dad acts hurt and rubs his head. Pouting, he looks up at Ruth: "Is that a no?"

Ruth snaps it most certainly is a NO!

My dad puts his arm around me, squeezes me hard, and

says, "OK, Ruth, if you won't run off with me, then how about my boy Josh here? Whaddya say?" Staring down at me, Ruth gives me a hug herself, a memory I'll cherish forever.

"Nah. Just a little too young. Maybe next year." Then she winks at me and walks off to place our order.

I always love this little show, or any of my Dad's other acts that bring smiles to the faces of everyone in the room. That's my dad.

But this lunch seems different than the others. For the first time I see some real tension coming from Al, and even my dad, too.

"Look, Al, you wanted to be president of the Police Union, and you got your wish. I still can't believe, though, that a bunch of Polacks and rednecks elected the only Jew on the force as their leader. Anti-Semites used to exhibit much better taste."

"You're the one that convinced me to join you down here in beautiful Hammond, Indiana. You said they'd love me. The only reason I got elected union president is because I'm the only one smart enough to see that the police chief and his drunken-bum, insurance salesman of a brother are screwing us."

My dad slumps down in the booth. I'm thinking it's the first time I've ever seen him look frustrated, but Al just keeps going.

"The cops in this town have got to have the worst policy and benefits on earth, thanks to Ronnie, and the chief is probably in on it. I've been asking around, and the firefighters and the rest of the city workers have it pretty bad too. Ronnie has a lock on insurance sales to anyone connected with the city. They get an extra cut from everybody's paycheck, and the cops wind up with lousy insurance coverage and a worthless retirement plan. So the other cops figured, 'Hey, maybe the Jew can do something about it.'"

I'm feeling like this isn't the kind of conversation that a ten-year-old is supposed to listen to, but that doesn't seem to be bothering my dad. I think he actually wants me to hear what's going on.

"Chief Wellstone isn't the kind of guy who is just going to roll over for you. And his brother is just plain mean. I mean *pull the wings off a fly mean*. You might be messing with the wrong guys here. Besides, the rest of the cops are going to keep hating you anyway. So what do you care?"

"So, what? I should just give up and let the chief and Ronnie keep screwing us?"

Dad leans forward and even cracks a small grin. He picks up the rabbit's foot from the table and dangles it in Al's face.

"No, I didn't say that was your only option. You could also consider shooting them in the ass. You got me pretty good. If my lucky rabbit's foot hadn't deflected *your* lousy bullet, I might be walking around today with a smaller pecker than you, and little Josh here wouldn't ever have seen the light of day." He says the last line a little louder for Ruth's benefit as she serves us our burgers.

"Your plan is I should just shoot the chief of police in the ass, and then they'll let us get a decent insurance plan?"

Dad's face grows darker, and in a rare moment of seriousness he says, "Al, really. Just let it go. These are bad guys, and they are holding all the cards. Okay? Let it go."

Al wipes his face with his napkin and gets up from the table. Where Ruth's breasts once held ground in front of my face, Al's enormous police revolver is now right at eye level, and I can't help but stare at it.

"Sorry. A little late for that. I already told the chief that I'm getting proposals for new coverage next week."

My dad let out a deep breath. "Just be careful. Don't get in over your head."

Al gives me a weak smile and turns to leave, but then stops to ask, "What time next Sunday?

"Come by a little before noon. The game starts at 1:00. Susan said to tell you she is looking forward to seeing Rebecca and the kids, and she'll help keep everybody busy while you and me and Josh watch the Bears kick Detroit's ass."

Putting his arm around my shoulder, Dad pulls me closer. "One more win and we're in the championship. Right, buddy?"

I feel like I'm going to explode with joy. We're flying high. Dad and I have watched every Bears game together all season, and now we're so close to being the champions of the National Football League. If you grow up in Chicago, you don't see a lot of championships come around. Football, baseball, whatever. Dad always says in Chicago the only guys who win every year are the local politicians.

I think that's why he is so worried about Al. It's kind of like Chief Wellstone and his brother, Ronnie, are the New York Giants or the Yankees, and Al is the Bears or the White Sox. Not a fair fight, but my dad always pulls for the underdog anyway.

Go, Bears, go.

4

Eighty-Six Hours before Sarah's Death

So far, so good. Twenty-seven minutes from our front door to Washington National Airport and a parking space less than five minutes' walk to the terminal. The only hairy part was the cab ride from the Nassau Airport across a fairly rural part of the island. Honestly, when Sarah and I got off the plane, I was expecting to see some guy in a suit standing next to a shiny black car and holding a sign with our name on it. Well, guess what— no guy, no sign, no shiny black car. So we piled into a dented van with four other couples for the fourteen-mile ride over to Paradise Island, and we all gasped in horror whenever our driver (who had an American car with the steering wheel on the left) would pass a truck on the two-lane, winding roads where they drive British-style *on the wrong side of the road!* But even in the van I could tell this was going to be a great weekend, as our fellow travelers were fairly well split between the burgundy and gold of the Redskins and the ridiculous aquamarine and orange of the Dolphins.

This is the first time that Sarah and I have been to Paradise Island, and in fact, with all of my work, it is one of the few trips we've taken alone in our ten years of marriage.

There wasn't much to see on the ride from the airport. We had a brief glimpse of Fort Charlotte, where the British flag had been lowered only ten years earlier when the Bahamas declared their independence, but the view from the top of the bridge that connected Paradise Island to Nassau was amazing, and the little island looked pristine. I planned, in addition to seeing the Skins kill the Dolphins and seeing myself killing the casino at craps, to take a walk on the beautiful beach where the James Bond movie *Thunderball* had been shot nearly twenty years before.

As our van pulls up in front of the Britannia Beach Hotel, I fall in love. Even Sarah, whose head has been killing her from the moment the plane took off, seems excited. I see why there was no shiny black car waiting for us at the airport. They are all in front of the Britannia Beach, and the couples who are being dropped off and welcomed seem to be just dripping with money. These people are definitely high rollers, who will be winning or losing more money in the next couple of days than most people earn in a year.

Coming into the hotel, I see long lines of guests checking in. It's kind of fun taking Sarah by the arm and walking to the open reservation desk marked "VIP Casino Guests Only."

"Yes, sir, may I help you?" This guy's tone of voice, especially with his clipped British accent, leaves no doubt that he's sure Sarah and I must be standing in the wrong line. Bainsworth is his name according to the tag on his jacket. John Bainsworth.

"Brown. Josh Brown. I'm an invited guest of the casino."

"Very well, sir. Let me just check our VIP list. I know most of our invited guests personally, and I don't recall seeing your name." He starts leafing through some printed pages, running his finger down the lists and shaking his head no, all the while making this annoying clicking sound with his teeth. "Gotta be a Dolphins fan," I whisper to Sarah. Finally, he flashes a nice big smile when he confirms that my name isn't anywhere on the list of invited guests. At the same time, he's looking over my shoulder at a "real" invited guest and motioning with his hands that he'll be just another minute chasing off the riff-raff.

"Okay, hold on. Sarah, can I have the letter from the hotel?" Sarah reaches into the beach bag that is doubling as an oversized purse and pulls out our travel documents. She passes the invitation letter directly to the reservation manager, who holds it in his fingertips like it had just come from the bottom of a birdcage. Letter in hand, he excuses himself to the now-impatient couple standing behind us and goes through a door into a private office.

A minute later he returns with a smirk on his face. "Mr. Brown, there seems to be some confusion about how and why this letter was sent to you, but we have a room for you in our sister hotel, The Loews, which you can access through the hallway right behind you. We will have a bellman accompany you, and my staff will call over to let them know you are on your way."

I start to argue that I don't want to stay in any "sister hotel," but Sarah gives my arm a familiar squeeze and says, "Please, Josh, let's just go. My head is killing me, and I've got to lie down." So off we go.

I'm not imagining things when I say that every step away from the Britannia Beach and toward The Loews is measured in carpeting that's a little less plush and walls that are a little more faded. Same for the guests. Some of them probably don't earn much more money than a lot of Grand National's policyholders. Just who I want to be hanging out with! But Sarah and I march on until our bellman points out the elevator we'll be taking up to the third floor. Sarah, looking pretty pale, turns to me with a weak smile and says, "Well, at least we made the third floor. They could have put us on two." To which the bellman, through a huge smile and in his soothing Bahamian accent, advises, "Ma'am, dere is no secund flor."

To add insult to injury, while we're standing there waiting for the elevator, we're joined by two clowns in Dolphins colors, each one topped off with a stupid yellow bumblebee antenna hat that's a dopey tribute to their defense, the so-called Killer B's. One of them, obviously a genius, elbows the other after examining my Redskins hat and shirt, and I hear him murmur under his breath, "Killer bees gonna sting your butts," followed by some honest-to-God giggling.

I'm ready to unload on the guy. Data is my life, so I ought to be able to bury him. Turning full-on, I stare him down and give him the bad news.

"You are going to lose. And let me tell you why you are going to lose. Your Killer B's have a cute name, but having six defensive players whose names all start with B is no match for the team ranked number one in lowest points scored by an opponent, and that's the Skins. You can pass, but Woodley is only averaging 54.7% to Theismann's 63.9%. Look at the facts," I bellow, quickly ticking them off on my fingers:

"Number One: You guys won't be able to handle Mike Nelms in an open field. He's rung up 809 yards returning both kickoffs and punts. Your guys have only 595 yards combined.

"Number Two: Mark Mosley is 20 for 21 in field goals, and there's talk he could become the first placekicker ever to be named the NFL MVP of the year.

"Number Three: Wayne Sevier is a former quarterback, so he knows how to run a whole unit like special teams.

"Number Four: Coach Sevier graduated from San Diego State with a degree in mathematics. With *distinction!* Coach Crosby graduated from Fort Hays State with degrees in phys ed.

"Enough said?"

The Dolphins fan on the receiving end of my attack finally manages to close his mouth after a few ill-fated attempts at stuttering. His friend mumbles that they should get out of here and wanders off, presumably looking for the nearest bar.

As we get on the elevator with the bellman trailing us, Sarah turns to me with a look of complete confusion.

"Josh, I thought Joe Gibbs was the coach of the Redskins. Who is Coach Sevier?"

"You've got to be kidding me. Coach Wayne Sevier heads up our special teams. You know, the kicking and punt return teams—critical stuff—and he is going to make the difference in us winning the Super Bowl. Jeez."

"Sorry for being so clueless, but if Coach Sevier is the Redskins' special teams coach, and I guess Coach Crosby is Miami's special teams coach, then who is Coach Berger?"

The elevator opens after our short ride up one level, and we follow the bellman as he opens the door to our room.

"Coach Berger? I have no idea who Coach Berger is. There is no Coach Berger, Sarah."

"Yes there is, Josh. Coach Michael Berger. He is in his late thirties, he is a pediatric dentist, his wife's name is Jody, and he has three kids of his own. I don't know any of his stats, but I do know he is your son's Pee Wee League football coach. You ought to check him out. And while you're at it, you can check out Coach Karen Cardinal, who is directing Sophie's Presidents' Day recital at the preschool next month. I *know* she has killer stats. Hasn't lost a kid yet."

I never saw it coming. Never even heard the footsteps. Just WHAM! Right upside my head.

That was the first shot. The next is walking into our room. Actually, it is more like a closet, with an eye-level view of the air-conditioning boxes mounted on the roof of the hotel lobby. I must have been in a state of shock, because before I can object, the bellman is closing the door behind him without even waiting for a tip.

Sarah has already kicked off her shoes and is lying on the bed, her eyes and forehead cupped under both hands and her face taut with pain, a look I've grown to recognize, even though she seldom complains. I can't help feeling really sad for her, even after the sucker punch she just gave me. I sit down with a heavy thump in the flimsy chair that, along with a cracked desk and a bed, are the only furnishings in this pathetic excuse for a room.

I think I must've even started to close my eyes too, because I jump when the room phone begins to clang.

Good, maybe it's the front desk with an upgrade from this dump.

I grab the receiver as Sarah reflexively turns on her side, away from the noise. "Hello?"

"Hello, Mr. Brown. It's Anthony Scappelli. Sorry to bother you on your vacation, but I just got another call from the same man who called before. He told me to call you at this number. He said I should tell you about the lawyer who is going to help me and the other policyholders. He said you would want to know."

Now I know I'm in shock. I take the phone from my ear and stare at it in complete disbelief.

"Mr. Brown? Mr. Brown? I'm begging you."

I don't hear the rest. I set the receiver down in its cradle and gently lie down on top of the bedspread next to Sarah so as not to disturb her. Who would have given this guy our home phone number? And now the hotel number? And, I'll have to deal with some lawyer of his.

Sherry has this number. I'm going to kill her! Or maybe it's some smart ass back in the office? Somebody's head is going to roll.

5

Seven Days before My Father Dies

Sammy Johnson and I have been best friends for as long as I can remember. When we were babies, our families were next-door neighbors, and I suppose we were all very close back then. Six years ago, Sammy's mother had to move the family. Sammy and his big sister, Beth, that is. They moved a few miles away into a small home soon after his father left them, but Sammy and I are still in the same school. We sit next to each other in Mrs. Archer's fifth-grade class, and we play together every day after school.

Anyway, it's not Sammy's fault. I blame his dad. I've heard the stories. And I used to see Mr. Johnson come home so drunk he could barely stand up. I'd see Mrs. Johnson crying. I'd see Beth as an angry twelve-year-old, and I'd watch Sammy eat and eat and eat until all the kids started calling him Dumbo, but like I said, it's not Sammy's fault.

I don't know for sure who was the first kid to call Sammy Dumbo, but if I had to guess, I'd say it was Mickey Wellstone. Mickey's father, Ronnie, is the man my dad warned Al about, and whenever I tell my dad about Mickey picking on Sammy, he makes a face like he has a stomachache and says, "Like father, like son." And Mickey is always bragging about how his uncle is the chief of police, and that he can have anybody arrested if he wants to.

But today is the worst. Sammy and I are throwing my football around behind the school and generally having a great time acting out Sunday's big game. Tough to do in winter parkas, but hey, we're good at pretending. Sammy beat me in paper, rock, scissors, so I have to be Detroit, and Sammy gets to be the Bears. He is loving every minute of it, because he already knows that he will, of course, win. I can't remember the last time I've seen Sammy this happy. That is, until Mickey and three of his buddies show up.

"Look, guys, it's Dumbo and his little friend. How are you girls doing today?"

By now Sammy is pretty used to this treatment, so he tries to ignore it, but I can see in his face how much it hurts. I guess that today insults alone aren't enough for Mickey, so he starts to kick Sammy in the rear end to the amusement of his lame-brained gang of buddies. "Look, guys, maybe I can kick Dumbo through the goal post and get a field goal for the Bears!"

I'm not the bravest kid in school, and it takes all I have inside me to say, "Come on, Mickey. We're not bothering you guys. How about leaving us alone now?"

"*Us*? Why are you saying *us*, Brown?" Mickey is moving away from Sammy now and heading within punching range of me. "Does this fat little pig belong to you, Brown? My uncle says the Johnsons are nothing but trash that needs to be put out. My uncle says Dumbo's father is a drunk and his big sister has become a whore who lives with a criminal. Is that the kind of friend you want, Brown? Because if it is, I'd love to knock your teeth right down your throat."

I guess I'm so focused on Mickey yelling and the fist he's waving in my face that I don't see one of his buddies sneaking around behind me. When Mickey starts pushing me hard in the chest, his partner bends down so that with one last hard push, Mickey has me tumbling backward over his pal and landing hard on my head on the frozen grass of the ball field.

From my poor vantage point on the ground, I can see legs all around me, and I hear the laughing. But suddenly this loud animal-like scream pierces the air, and we all turn to see where it's coming from. Mickey's a second too late as Sammy, like a charging bull, catches him square in the stomach with a head butt.

I start to sit up when I see Mickey literally go flying through the air, coming to rest in some slushy, black snow. For a moment Mickey just lies there stunned, and there's complete silence. Everybody, including Sammy, has their mouths open and seems to be frozen in time. Then Mickey begins to come around. He gets halfway up, his face turning red as he screams, "You're dead, Johnson! Let's get this fat boy!"

In a flash Mickey and his three friends are all over Sammy. Before I know what's happening, they've knocked off his glasses and have him on the ground. Sammy is being hit so hard and fast that he can't even call my name, but our eyes meet and I see the saddest look I will probably ever see. I don't remember getting to my feet but I do remember grabbing my football and running. Not so much running to anyplace at all as just running to get away from Mickey and his friends. If I have any thought at all, it's to get out of there as fast as I can.

I don't stop running until I get home. Taking the key out from under the doormat, I let myself in. It's after four o'clock, and my parents will be home in another hour or so. I think maybe if I wash up and change clothes, my folks won't find out what happened today. Maybe it will all just go away.

I tell myself those guys wouldn't really hurt Sammy, and anyway, if I'd stayed, we both would have gotten clobbered. What would be the good in that? Sammy will understand.

I'm pretty quiet all through dinner. When my mom asks if anything is wrong, I tell her I just have a headache. When my dad teases me that he can't remember the last time I was this quiet, I tell him that my throat hurts a little too. I'm actually glad when my mom says I should take a hot bath and go to bed early so as not to miss school tomorrow. I have to go, too, because tomorrow is the last day to turn in my parents' permission slip so that I can attend the fifth-grade overnight sledding trip to Wisconsin. Sammy and I used to sled down the little hill right in our own front yards, and I'm really looking forward to this trip, my first ever away from my parents. I was hoping Sammy would go too, but he said his mom doesn't have the money. Maybe after what happened today it's just as well. I can picture Mickey and his friends coming after us in their sleds until they catch us in the woods and beat the crap out of us.

I keep thinking of Sammy just lying there on the ground with those guys punching and kicking him. Looking at Sammy and seeing him just looking at me. Not calling out for help, just looking. Looking until I got up and ran as fast as I could back to my house.

Lying in bed, I see the outline of my dad in the doorway. "You're crying. And it's not your head, and it's not your throat. When you want to tell me what it is, I'm right here." I feel the bed sag a little as he sits on the edge and pushes the hair out of my wet eyes. I think I take my dad by surprise, sitting up so quickly and hugging him as hard as I can.

"What's the matter? What's wrong?"

I just keep hugging him like I'm never going to let go. I can't tell my dad what happened because I'm too ashamed. I can't bear the thought of my dad not being proud of me because I ran away. Ran like a scared little puppy dog, leaving my best friend all alone when he needed me most.

"Did something bad happen at school?"

Well, I have to tell him something.

"Sammy and I were playing football after school, and these guys started picking on him. It was Mickey Wellstone and some of his friends."

"They were picking on Sammy again because he's fat?"

"Yeah. And because he doesn't have a father. Because Mr. Johnson drank too much and just left them. Now they tease Sammy because Beth has run away, and Mickey's uncle says she's a whore and living with some kind of criminal. They even make fun of the little house that Sammy and his mom live in, and sometimes they throw stones at their windows."

"What happened today, son? What did those guys do to you and Sammy?"

I just couldn't tell him.

"We got scared and we ran away from them. We just ran."

"Josh, let me tell you about Sammy's father. It's true, he did drink too much, and when he did, nobody in town would give him a job, so he was humiliated and he left. But deep down he is a good man. When the Johnsons lived next door, I got to know him pretty well. You know that he was in the war, just like me."

Dad pauses for a moment and seems to be just looking off into space.

"War is a horrible thing, Josh, and lots of horrible things happened to some very good people. I know that Al and I joke about it all the time, but a lot of good people never came back from the war, and even some of us who did come back have never been the same again. Of course Mickey's father, and even his uncle, would never know that, because neither of them ever saw any combat.

"Josh, I know you and Sammy ran away today, but remember, there will always be another Mickey around the corner who wants to tell you what to do. The thing is, there won't always be another Sammy there. Having a friend like Sammy is a real gift. You think about it, Josh. You're a good boy, and I know you'll do the right thing—now, and when you're a dad yourself."

"I can't go on the trip to Wisconsin. Those guys will beat me up for sure."

"You can't run away either. I'm not going to let you. You are going on that trip, and I'll make sure that Sammy has the money to go too. Look at it this way: you and Sammy are the Bears; Mickey and his friends are the Detroit Lions. Just do your best, and always stand by your friends when they are in the right." Then, kissing me on my forehead, Dad ends the conversation the way he almost always does, with a broad smile and the words, "Tomorrow will be a better day. Don't worry, son. Just go out and have yourself some fun."

Right then, at ten years old, I know what I want to be when I grow up. I want to be my dad. I just don't know if I can be. My dad would never have left his friend and run away.

6

Eighty Hours before Sarah's Death

To say the least, this weekend isn't turning out the way I expected. Dinner was awful, hitting bottom with an undercooked lobster for me and a burned-to-a-crisp steak for Sarah. All that plus a stuffy captain who insisted I take off my Redskins hat in the restaurant. Good thing this trip is free. Otherwise, dinner would have been thirty-five dollars for nothing! But, I'm already down more than a hundred bucks in craps, so maybe the casino won't be the only loser on this trip.

Sarah tried a little blackjack at the five-dollar table, but quit when she lost the first three hands she was dealt. She took a roll of nickels out of her purse and headed over to the slot machines along the wall, but it wasn't more than fifteen minutes later when she came to find me rolling the dice. Of course, I threw a losing 7 the moment she walked up to the table, but she only wanted to let me know her head was pounding and she needed to go to bed. I guess I sounded a little insincere when I asked her if she needed me to walk her back to our little dump of a room. So she let me off the hook with a weak smile and a plea not to lose *too much.*

I've only played craps once before, last year in Las

47

Vegas, when my boss invited me to join him at a meeting with our top-selling agents. We just walked up to an empty table at Caesar's Palace. Phil—he told me to call him Phil now—gave me $100 in chips. Then he put $10 on the pass line for me, right next to his own green $25 chip, and he proceeded to roll the dice. But only for two rolls, until the dreaded 7 came up instead of the 6 we needed to win. We were still the only two players at the table when he motioned for the stickman to pass me the dice, and he announced to no one in particular, "Virgin roller, boys. Mortgage the farm!"

By the time I was done rolling, about twenty-five minutes later, our table had filled up with gamblers drawn over by my boss . . . er, my buddy . . . Phil's screaming. I was up more than $1,200, and Phil must have made at least $10,000. When the losing 7 finally came up and my roll was over, Phil was quick to cash us both out, reminding me that we were winners. Taking the house's money was the name of the game, *not* giving it back. Appropriate attitude for the head of a large insurance company, I suppose.

The next day in Vegas was filled with meetings and then a redeye flight back to D.C. So, my one and only experience at the crap table taught me two things: first, it was the most exciting game I had ever played, and second, maybe I'm not so unlucky after all. But that was Las Vegas last year, and nothing about this trip is going well, so no surprise that the money is all flowing one way from me to the house. Glad Phil isn't here to see this. He's not big on losers.

Some vacation this is turning out to be! And some *VIP treatment.* No car at the airport, a dumpy room with no view, Sarah's headaches are worse than ever, the food is lousy, and the dice are ice-cold. What else can possibly go wrong? As soon as I think that, my hand shoots reflexively up to my Redskins hat. No! That's where the bad vibes have to stop. The Skins are going to win this thing, and I'll be here to watch it.

For a craps player, there is nothing worse than a quiet table. It means that not only are you a loser, but you are standing around with a bunch of strangers who are losers too. Just my idea of a good time: hanging out with a bunch of losers. Long faces, painful grimaces, occasional groans, and . . . is that laughing? Somebody here thinks this is fun? So yeah, I'm pretty surprised when I hear people start laughing. I mean absolutely howling, and only a few feet away from me. Where did they come from, anyway? And how long have they been standing there?

Strange crowd too. I see two beautiful women in cocktail dresses who could pass for movie stars. Then there are a couple of older guys in suits who are clearly made of money. But it's not those guys, or even the beautiful women, that catch my eye. It's another man right in the center of it all who seems to be holding court, much to the delight of his companions. I can't get a close look at his face because of the crowd gathered on all sides, but what I can see is beyond strange. Like the other men in his group, he is wearing an immaculate coat and tie, but if that weren't odd enough for the laid-back Bahamas, what is really strange is that this man's dapper outfit is topped off by, of all things, a Chicago Bears hat! In a sea of Redskins and Dolphins logos and colors, this character is wearing the blue and orange that I used to know so well. What a nut!

His friends call him Robert, and they are loving the show he is working for them. Through all the laughing I catch a few words of the story he is spinning, but I'm more interested in the rack full of black and pink chips he has in front of him. Calculating that each black chip is worth $100 and each pink one is $500, my quick math tells me this guy must have more than $50,000 in front of him. It's pretty obvious, too, that he is unaware, or at least totally uninterested, in the craps game—he's simply putting fresh chips down with each losing roll without so much as a glance at the table or the action of those ice-cold dice. Strange, too, I think as I look around our mostly empty table, that nobody else seems even to notice the group at the end of the table.

I guess I'm so taken with this remarkable scene that I hardly notice when another losing 7 wipes out the small remainder of my chips. Okay, granted, I've only played craps once before, but I came to the table very cocky that I would repeat my Vegas streak. Still, I had hit my self-imposed nightly limit of $200 in losses.

On the other hand, maybe I can still turn my luck around.

I take out my wallet and do a quick count of what I have left. I'm down to my last $250 in cash. As I pull out a crisp $100 bill, I promise myself that this will be the last of my wagers for tonight. I drop the bill onto the green felt, waiting for the stickman to give me a fresh supply of chips, when a voice, his voice, cuts right through to my heart.

"Tomorrow will be a better day, son."

His eyes. His eyes bore right into me. His friends have all backed away and are talking softly amongst themselves. Now I can't take my eyes off him.

"Pick up your money, son. Tomorrow will be a better day. I promise."

I'm too numb to say anything. I just pick up my money and nod. He rewards me with a quick smile. You could call him a nice-looking man, of average height and build, with silver hair at the temples, as befits someone probably approaching sixty. Then he just nods at me one more time and flashes that brilliant smile. Staring all the while. Staring like he can look right into my heart. Then in a flash he turns away and is immediately swallowed up by his adoring friends, who are begging for another story.

Slowly I walk away from the table and head back to the room. But as I'm leaving, I swear I can hear him say, "Just have yourself some fun."

I don't even remember walking back to the room. My head is spinning. What just happened back there? How is this possible? I reach into my pocket for my room key and realize through my daze that I must have left it in the room. The last thing I want to do is disturb Sarah from what I know must be a fitful sleep, but I have no choice. Quietly at first, but then excitedly and loudly enough to wake the dead, I pound on the door.

7

Six Days before My Father Dies

I'm told the pounding on the door sounded like cannon fire.

Al Kaplan is a pretty sound sleeper. His wife and kids less so, but nobody could have slept through the pounding on his front door. Wondering briefly whether to grab his service revolver, he thought the better of it and pulled on his bathrobe. He groaned as Rebecca ran to the kids' room to comfort their crying.

Opening the door a crack, he was rewarded with a beam of light shot directly into his eyes, temporarily blinding him. A moment later, he was pushed aside and nearly knocked to the ground as the door flew open under the force of three huge county sheriff's officers. In a heartbeat they took him down, one with a knee to the back of his neck, the other holding down his head by his ears and hair. A third grabbed his wrists and cuffed him behind his back.

None of them spoke a word, and Rebecca's screams cut through the air before she could shield the kids from the horrible scene. Al was bleeding now from behind his left ear, where he had been clubbed on his way down to the ground. He didn't get a very good look at the sheriff's

53

officers, but he thought he recognized one or two of them from occasional visits to the county seat in Crown Point.

Mostly what he felt was pain, a searing pain in his right wrist where the handcuff was cutting into his skin. He could hear Rebecca sobbing now and yelled out "Leave her alone!" to the officer that was pushing her back.

The sergeant leading the group got down on one knee and put his face right in Al's.

"Kaplan, you are a disgrace to anyone who wears the uniform of a law enforcement officer. Today is a very black day for us all, and we owe it all to you. Al Kaplan, you are under arrest for rape and assault. Anything you say can and will be used against you."

He didn't hear the rest. He didn't have to. They had him on his feet and halfway out the door before he could even react. He could only hope that Rebecca and the kids would be all right and that Rebecca had heard his pleas to wake up Bob. He and Bob had been getting each other out of tight spots since they were in grade school. And he prayed Bob could figure this one out too.

He barely made out the officers' words now as they opened the door to the patrol car. "Oh, resisting arrest too, huh?" The blow to the middle of his stomach knocked the air out of him, but it was the club to the back of his head that threw him into darkness.

———————

The ringing phone wakes me from my sleep and, in a daze, I walk to my parents' room just as my mom hands over the phone to Dad.

"Bob, get up. It's Rebecca, and she's hysterical. She says Al was beaten and taken off by some sheriff's officers."

There is not much that bothers my dad, and little that can get him up and out of bed in the middle of a cold winter night, but he jumps up and into a pair of slacks in one motion. I think he would have run out the door and into the frozen night barefoot if my mom hadn't slowed him down a little with some logic and a few good questions.

"What can Al have done that the sheriff's officers would break into his house in the middle of the night and take him away like that?"

"Al didn't do anything—nothing except mess with the wrong people. And they couldn't send in the Hammond cops because they couldn't control what might happen with Al's own guys in the room. My guess is Chief Wellstone set this up and got some of his pals in the county to help him out."

Now Dad has his shoes on, shirt, belt. Looking down from the top of the stairs, I see Mom following right behind Dad as he opens the hall closet, reaching for his coat and hat.

"I'm going to Crown Point, Sue. They must have taken Al to the sheriff's lockup. I'll call you when I know what's going on. Call Rebecca and tell her not to worry. Tell her they are not going to get away with this. Tell her I give her my word."

They hug briefly, then he is gone. When Dad opens the front door, I see icy sleet reflected in the streetlights and feel the blast of cold air even at the top of the stairs, where I'm standing in my pajamas. But I'm not scared; I know my dad will make everything all right. I actually smile as I slip back to bed without my mom even telling me I have to.

I can hear my parents' voices coming from the kitchen as I come downstairs for breakfast. Peeking around the corner, I see that Dad is still wearing the same clothes he ran out the door in, and he hasn't shaved or even brushed his hair. I duck my head back quickly because I want to hear what my dad is saying, and I know it isn't anything meant for my ears.

"They have him in a filthy cell, Sue, down in their basement, and he's been beat up pretty good. The story they are floating is that Al was cruising alone last night and came upon a car with its motor running and its windows all steamed up, just parked somewhere in a pretty deserted area. They say that Al found these two kids in the backseat of the car, and they had goods with them that looked to be stolen or something. The story goes that Al scared off the boy, then got in the backseat himself and raped the girl."

I hear my mother retch, and I peek again as she settles herself back down. She asks, "But why Al? How can they blame this on Al?"

My dad looks like he is going to be sick himself, and for a moment he just sits there staring out the kitchen window, saying nothing.

"I think it's Beth, honey. Beth Johnson. The sheriff's office wouldn't tell me much, but I did hear that it was a local girl, seventeen, they said, who'd run away from home. We've all heard that Beth is gone, that either she ran away from home or Roberta finally threw her out to protect Sammy. I guess she's been hanging around with the wrong crowd, and her latest boyfriend is a real loser. But she is only seventeen. I wonder if she's a minor? They say Al slapped her around and raped her right in the back of that car—a stolen car, by the way.

"Beth knows Al, she grew up around him, so even though it was nighttime and there wasn't much light, she made a definite ID, and then when they dragged Al into the lockup, she ID'd him again."

My next peek around the corner might have been one too many. I see my mother looking as white as new snow with her hand clamped over her mouth. Maybe, I don't know for sure, but maybe my dad saw me this time, so I quickly turn and tiptoe upstairs. I stop dead in my tracks, though, when I hear my mom ask, "Bob, you don't think . . . I mean, you don't think Al is guilty?"

"I don't need to think about this. I *know* what happened. They can say anything they want. Al could never do this. No, this is payback from the chief and Ronnie. I just have to help Al prove it."

I feel so bad for Sammy. All the teasing he is already getting from Mickey and the other kids, and now if they ever find out that his sister got caught up in more bad stuff, it will be even worse. And Mickey will love this. Everybody knows that Al is my dad's best friend, but Mickey's uncle is the chief of police, and he always says that his uncle can have anybody he wants arrested. Well, maybe he can.

I'm afraid for myself, but I think I'm even more afraid for Sammy and what they might do to him next. Then I think about my dad and what he is doing for his friend Al . . . and I remember Sammy. Sammy, lying on the ground getting beat up while I get up and run away. I feel so ashamed, but I resolve right then and there to be a better friend. No matter what.

A lot of this problem with Al doesn't make sense to me, but I know one thing for sure: my dad doesn't believe that Al has done anything wrong, so neither do I.

Later that day, Dad takes some money out of the bank and bails Al out of jail. I think my mom is scared about the whole thing, and at dinner that night I learn that Dad is going to give Al a job at Lucky Auto, and why he has to.

My mom is small and her hand looks so tiny when she rests it on Dad's arm.

"You know there isn't anything for Al to do at the store. James runs the place perfectly. Besides, how are we going to pay him?"

Dad puts his other hand on top of hers.

"Sue, they have suspended him without pay until after the trial, and who knows when that is going to be. Al and Rebecca need our help. There isn't anybody else." Then my dad gets that silly little smile on his face that we all know so well.

"Besides, don't you want to see the look on Al's face when I tell him he will be reporting to a colored man? You know, for a Jew he's not the most liberal guy in the world, and on top of that, when we were in the army, he hated the officers. Now he'll be working for a retired colored officer fifteen years his junior. That's going to be worth the price of admission alone!"

That's my dad. Fires burning all around and he not only jumps in, he's laughing all the way.

8

Sixty-Six Hours before Sarah's Death

The towels we grabbed next to the pool are enough to cover the lounge chairs, but I am tempted to get a few more to use as blankets. The day is clear and sunny, and through the windows of the hotel coffee shop, it looked beautiful by the pool, but another twenty degrees sure wouldn't hurt anybody. Still, things are looking up!

"I don't think I've ever seen you like this," Sarah says. "I mean, I love that you are so excited, but listen to yourself. You are the most logical man in the world, and you aren't making any sense!"

I lean forward in the lounge chair and set down the book I haven't even cracked.

"I know it doesn't make any sense, but you have to meet him. You never knew my dad, but this guy looks just like I remember him, other than being twenty or thirty years older. It's his eyes and his smile. And the way that everyone around him just loves him. It's just—I don't know—it's just incredible."

One thing about Sarah, she can be fighting a doozy of a headache but still care only about me and the kids. She reaches over and takes my hand.

"Can I tell you something? I'm not a psychologist, but

just before we left the house, your mom called to talk about your dad. It's Super Bowl weekend, and your dad died just before the championship game, and you're obviously thinking about it. It's only natural. You won't admit it, but you miss him so much, and when this nice man, who is about the age your dad would be, starts talking to you, something clicks. Come on, Josh! You're Mr. Logic. You're Mr. Data. Get a grip!"

Well, right now I'm not Mr. Logic. Or Mr. Data. I am a giant balloon, and Sarah is letting the air out with each word she speaks.

"I know, I know. It's just that this man is so much like my dad."

Sarah smiles that sad smile she does so well when Richie or Sophie is crying. I just nod. There isn't anything more I can say. I sit back in the lounge chair and, in vain, pick up my book one more time. After reading the same page three times, I have to admit that I just can't focus. The bigger surprise is that I am not even interested in the *Miami Herald* sports section all about tomorrow's Super Bowl, which I'd grabbed in the lobby. I try the water in the pool, getting only as far as my big toe, and that doesn't do it for me either. Next I reach for the latest data analysis reports from Grand National that I'd brought along, and even those, my old friends, leave me restless beyond reason. After another half hour of fighting sheer antsy-ness, I get to my feet.

"Where are you off to, mister?"

"Just a little exploring, honey. Want to join me?"

Sarah can tell it isn't a very sincere offer. "You mean the casino, right?" As I reach into her beach bag for my wallet, she adds, "Just don't lose too much money, and be back by 1:00 for lunch."

My quick kiss to her forehead causes her a flicker of pain, reminding me without words that she still isn't quite right. I smile and stroll away, slowly at first, but once I'm out of her sight, I practically have to stop myself from running like a halfback who sees daylight through the defensive line. But what is drawing me forward? Is it the crap table and the chance to get back my $200, or something else?

———————

Casinos are amazing places. Timeless. Literally. Of course there is never a clock on the wall, but it's not even noon, and the place looks exactly as it did when I left it the night before. With one exception. The casino is empty, practically a ghost town.

As I walk down the green-and-orange carpeted aisle past the first bank of nickel slots, I see a handful of semi-obese men and women with cigarettes dangling from their lips. Shit. I wonder how many of them have policies with Grand National? Then past the blackjack tables, including one that has just a two-dollar minimum. That will change by 5:00 p.m., when I'll be lucky to find a five-dollar table.

At first I'm afraid that the silence means there isn't even a crap table open, but there it is. And there *he* is, staring right through me with that great smile of his that I can spot even from a hundred feet away.

I'm not usually a very outgoing person. I mean, other than the Redskins—and my family, of course—to me most people are just data points on a graph. But this is different.

Or maybe it is his smile that makes me stick out my hand before I even reach the table.

"Well, we meet again," I say as I reach for my money with my other hand. "I'm Josh Brown."

His firm handshake is warm to the touch, and I feel a jolt, like electricity rushing through my body. "Hello, Josh. I'm Robert. Robert Saber."

Unreal. The eyes. The smile. Even a Bears hat. And his name.

"My father's name was Robert, but he always went by Bob."

"You said 'went by'? Did your father pass away?"

"Many years ago. I lost my dad, and the Bears lost one of their biggest fans. Although with you wearing that hat when they aren't even in Sunday's game, you might've given him a run for his money!"

"Do you miss him much?"

I try to answer, but the lump in my throat takes me by surprise, and I can't talk, so I just nod.

Robert smiles and leans in closer, saying, "Well, look, Josh. You've got your memories, but that's all in the past. Right now, you've got to get that pretty wife of yours feeling better."

And just like that the lump in my throat is gone.

"My wife? You don't know my wife. What do you mean I have to get her feeling better?"

Robert holds up both hands in mock surrender and his tanned face crinkles nicely as he smiles. "Wasn't that your wife who came up to you at the crap table last night? I'm a professional people-watcher, Josh, but it doesn't take a trained eye to see that she was feeling pretty bad."

I didn't think Sarah looked so bad last night, so I just shrug and say, "She had a little headache, that's all."

"I hope so. Just take care of your wife, and the rest will take care of itself."

The rest? What is he talking about *the rest?*

"Anyway, son, I think it's time to have ourselves some fun!"

"I hope you remember your promise to me."

"I haven't forgotten. I promised you last night that today would be a better day, and it will be. Besides," he says, motioning to the handful of pasty, lifeless old players glumly standing around the table, "maybe you'll be a real roller. The rest of these guys are dead."

Almost on cue the stickman slides the dice over to me, and I realize my hundred-dollar bill has been transformed into a stack of twenty orange five-dollar chips. Robert's rack isn't quite as impressive as it was last night, but he still has a fair number of black hundreds in front of him. He puts one of them on the pass line right in front of me and another thousand in front of his own position.

I look over at him in shock, but he just smiles and says, "Okay, son, let's have ourselves some fun!"

Now a word about the game of craps. There is no uglier number in craps than a 7, unless, of course, 7 is the first number rolled, in which case it's a winner. So when I roll a 7 three times in a row, well, let me just say that even the old stiffs at the other end of the table start to perk up a little. A few of them even get a little color back in their faces and *almost* crack a smile or two.

Robert persuades me to press the first $100 winner, and when the second one comes up, I am back up the $200 I was down. When the third 7 hits, I'm up $200. Just like that. I try to pay Robert back the original $100 he'd spotted me, but he's pretty pleased with the $1,000 he made with my first roll and pressed up to $4,000. So rather than take back the $100, he has me throw it on the spot for 11.

"OK, son, how about a YO? YO eleven." That is craps lingo for the beautiful 6 and 5 that always means WINNER, but as a table bet, it lasts for only one roll.

I give the dice a rattle in my upheld fist, then have Robert blow on them for good luck. The dice fly and a 6 hits first, but the second die just keeps spinning like a top. As it begins to slow, I can see that a second 6—a LOSER 12—is about to settle.

But dice are funny things. They have a life of their own, and when that die falls against the green felt bumper, up comes that beautiful 5. A beautiful 6 and 5, baby, at fifteen to one. That's $1,500 for the 11 and another $400 for the win on the pass line. And then, well, that's when the dice get really hot!

I start making my own bets of $500, and then go up to $1,000 on the pass line, with my *odds* bet of anywhere from $1,500 to $5,000, not to mention another $250 on each of the numbers. I watch in wonder as the chips in my rack bloom, turning from green to black to pink, and growing and growing until both rows are nearly full.

With each roll Robert and I, and now about twenty of our new closest friends, yell at the top of our lungs, "Come on 8. Let's see the 8; 4 and a 4! Now the 9. Let's go dice, 6 and a 3! Now a 5. Forty-one dice. WINNER! WINNER! WINNER! Pay the man, pay the man, PAY THE MAN!"

The whole thing takes only about thirty minutes, slightly longer than my daily commute into northwest D.C., but I now have more than fifty bones. That's more than $50,000 smiling back at me from the table. And Robert? Well, his bets have dwarfed mine, and when he starts getting above a couple hundred thousand dollars, a security guard slips in behind him, and by the time my roll ends, his rack of nearly $500,000 earns us a full escort over to the cashier's cage. We saunter over like the best of pals, with his arm slung lazily over my shoulder.

I suppose I've had a better half hour in my life, but don't ask me to tell you when it was, because nothing quite comes to mind. Anyway, Sarah is not going to believe this!

Robert says we have to have a celebratory drink, and since by now I've completely forgotten my promise to Sarah to be back by 1:00, it sounds like a pretty good plan to me, especially when we are escorted to the VIP lounge in the back of a private room reserved for special guests. I sink down into the soft black leather chair and don't even see the cocktail waitress walk up to our small table.

"What can I get for you gentlemen today?" Tough question coming from a slightly older but still very attractive blond whose Playboy Bunny–styled outfit barely covers her ample breasts. Interesting perfume too. Have I seen her before somewhere?

Robert grins and orders us each a cold beer. He smiles and says, "All the best things come in pairs." The waitress blushes a little when Robert says she is the most beautiful woman he has ever seen in his life and he'll be heartbroken if she doesn't walk down to the marina with him and sail off into the sunset.

She is pretty funny herself, and without breaking stride comes right back with, "I'm so sorry, sir, but you are just a little too old for me, like maybe thirty years or so."

Robert clasps his hands over his heart with great dramatic flair and throws his head back in mock desperation. He stays in that death-like pose for maybe a beat or two. When he comes out of it, he slips his arm around me and comes right back with, "Okay, if you won't go out with me, then how about my boy here?"

I turn beet red. The waitress makes a pretend swat at Robert through the air, gives us both a wink, and walks off to order our drinks. That was fun, a little strange for some reason, but fun.

I settle into the deep, soft leather chair and let out a contented sigh as I look over the elegant VIP lounge. When I look back over to Robert, I am surprised to see him leaning forward and staring intently into my eyes.

"Tell me about your wife. It's Sarah, right?"

Usually I'm a very private person, and my first reaction is not to reveal too much to him.

"Sarah? She's great. We met right after college when she was teaching and I was finishing law school. Great wife and a great mother to our little Richie and Sophie."

Robert's next question belies the warm smile on his face.

"That's it?"

"Sure. What else is there?"

"I asked you to tell me about her. You gave me her résumé."

He leans in even closer. "What's your special, magical connection? What makes the two of you a team? What is it that makes you think about her first thing every morning and last thing every night?"

I try to put him off with a smile of my own, but I don't think it's working. I jokingly ask, "Hey, am I being taped for *The Newlywed Game*? I don't know about the magical connection. I think she's pretty. She's nice. We only dated for about a year, and then we both wanted to get married and start our own family."

"Starting a family was important to you? That's why you got married?"

I only have to think about it for a moment.

"Yeah, I'd say that was it. Sarah lost both of her parents before she even finished high school. First her dad when she was very little, and then her mom when she was sixteen. Her big sister wound up pretty much raising her. So I'd say, yeah, Sarah really wanted to have a family."

His eyes never leave me for a minute. He doesn't even seem to blink.

"And you'd lost your father when you were only ten."

Funny, but I don't remember telling him how old I was when my dad died. My eyes are locked with his now, and I just nod, not knowing if I would be able to speak anyway.

Robert leans back and smiles, breaking the spell just as the hostess shows up with our beers. We clink our glasses together.

"You know, son, I don't think a beer is going to do justice to our celebration. How about if you let me take you and that pretty wife of yours to dinner tonight? I'm thinking Café Martinique at 8:00. Work for you?"

We make a date, and as we get up to leave, in walks my old friend from the hotel reservation desk, who still doesn't even know that I'm alive.

"Good afternoon, Mr. Saber. I understand from the casino manager that congratulations are in order. Well done! And I trust that everything is perfect with your suite?"

Robert flashes that great smile of his. "Perfect, Bainsworth, old man. Absolutely perfect."

Bainsworth gives a thin smile in response and even a bit of a bow to excuse himself, all without so much as a glance in my direction. As he turns to leave, Robert stops him short.

"Hold on there, Bainsworth. You didn't inquire about my boy here. How about it, Josh? Is your suite perfect too?"

The only way I can describe the look on the manager's face is *priceless,* as his brief recollection of me comes back into focus and the thin smile becomes lock-jawed with tension.

"Well, to tell you the truth, Mr. Bainsworth, my wife and I are just a little upset with our roomette over in the Loews tower. And you should warn your Maintenance Department that the air-conditioner casings are starting to rust out. The ones right in front of our window."

Bainsworth's brief spell of stuttering is relieved when Robert puts his arm around him and walks him a few feet away, whispering I don't know what into his ear. They briefly shake hands, and Bainsworth turns to leave, but only after he actually looks me in the eyes and gives me that silly little bow of his.

"Here's the plan," says Robert. "It's almost 1:00. Why don't you run off and get some lunch with your wife and spend a little time with her to make sure she's feeling better? Then we'll meet at 8:00 for dinner, and maybe for dessert we can wander back down to the crap table and kick a little ass."

"Sounds like a good plan to me." My goofy grin is becoming like a permanent fixture.

We shake hands again. God, his hands are warm. He catches my arm as I'm turning away.

"Oh, and save a little time to check in with the bell captain. I guess the hotel had a last-minute cancellation, and the room next to mine opened up, so my pal Bainsworth is bumping you up."

I shake my head in wonder. "How in the world did you do that?"

"It's easy, son. You just have to know how to talk to people."

9

Five Days before My Father Dies

Another Saturday at Lucky Auto, and it's almost time for lunch with my dad. My favorite time of the whole week. But even a ten-year-old can tell when things aren't quite right, and things at the store seem a little strange today.

The setup at Lucky Auto has always been pretty simple. My dad's job is to walk around and make everybody feel good, both the customers and the employees. My mom runs the "office," which is about the size of a large closet with two desks, a huge desktop calculator, and lots of files crammed in it. This means my mom is in charge of anything that has to do with money, like paying the bills or tallying up the day's sales. James runs the shop, where he supervises the work of eight to ten men, some of whom my dad says are highly skilled craftsmen, but none of whom can work harder than James.

I know that Mom and Dad are happy with how the business has grown in the last few years, and they even had to knock out the cinder-block back wall and add two more garages to keep up with the work. They mostly do things like seat covers and carpeting, work that my dad brings in from his car dealer and insurance agent friends.

I've even heard my mom and dad talking with James about opening up a second store and a warehouse over in East Chicago.

Today is Al's first day at Lucky Auto, and my dad is showing him around. Al has a bandage over his right ear and a pretty scary-looking black eye on the other side of his face, and he's walking with a newly acquired limp, courtesy of the sheriff's department.

I'm in the storeroom area between the showroom and the garages, taking inventory—a very important job for a ten-year-old, by the way—when they stop outside the door to talk before going back to where James and the others are hard at work. I can hear every word they say.

"Look, Rebecca and I will never be able to thank you enough for standing up for me and bailing me out, but you and I both know that my working here is a really bad idea. I mean, it feels like charity or something."

"Charity? When I turn you over to James for training and he starts to kick the shit out of you, you'll know it's not charity. We *work* here, pal. It's not like sitting around in a squad car all day eating doughnuts."

"Yeah, well, that's the other thing I need to talk to you about."

"You mean James?"

"Come on, Bob. Most of the jerks in this town think I raped some teenaged girl. Now they'll see me taking orders from a colored guy. You think I can fall any farther?"

I have to see this and peek around the corner. My dad smiles. "Well, at least now I finally understand how it came about that you shot me in the ass. You're an idiot, Al. A first-class idiot."

Al tries to look angry, but he just can't pull it off, and they both start laughing.

"Here's the thing," Dad continues. "Sue and I have had a good run the past couple of years with Lucky Auto, and we've been thinking about opening up a second store. Maybe if you let James train you, and you promise not to shoot any of the customers, things could just take care of themselves and you could wind up running the new place."

"Store manager? I like the sound of that. And then I'd be working for you, right? James wouldn't be my boss if I was a store manager, right?"

"No, that's not right. James has been with Sue and me for years. You know that. He was just a kid when his dad was killed, and I practically raised him myself; first some little odd jobs, and then more responsibility while he was still growing up. The kid put himself through college, and when he got home from Korea, medals and all, I told him I wanted him to come back to work for me and that he'd run the place. He's about the smartest guy I've ever met and he's loyal, too, just like other people I know. He is going to be your boss now, so you might as well get over it."

"If it weren't for you, I'd still be in the sheriff's lockup. I really owe you, and that's no bull. I'll do my best, but look, I know we are in modern times. I know it's 1956. Still . . . it isn't going to be easy working for a colored."

"Here's a tip for you. He's not 'a colored.' He's James Artis. Lieutenant James Artis, U.S. Army retired, and if you'll give him half a chance, he can teach you a thing or two."

I can see that Al is thinking it over. "And what if I try, really try, but it just doesn't work between the two of us?"

"Well, in that case, there's no problem."

"Really?"

"Yeah, really. 'Cause you'll be gone!" My dad lets out a true belly laugh as he takes Al by the arm and walks him back to James. I watch Al and James shake hands, but even I can tell that these men, the two men my dad likes the best, just don't get on.

My dad and James pride themselves on how they can understand each other so well without even talking half the time. Today, my dad just says, "Lieutenant Artis, I am assigning Private Kaplan to your unit. Sorry, lieutenant, but somebody has to take his pitiful ass. Now if you gentlemen will excuse me, it is almost noon, and I have an important strategy-planning session booked with my special assistant."

My dad turns to leave them, waving as always over his shoulder as he yells out, "Josh, get your coat. Gloves too. We have a lot of strategy to discuss."

———————

When we get to Giovanni's, I head for our usual front booth, but Dad walks right past and instead goes all the way to the back, where one man is sitting alone. Something else is different too. Instead of the usual hollering and teasing, my dad doesn't say a word. He just nods silently to Tony behind the counter as we walk by.

Dad shakes the hand of the man at the table. "Thanks for joining me, mayor. Especially at the last minute and all."

I'd seen the mayor a couple of times before, including at the celebration party after his election in November—his first win. I know my folks like him because for months we had a campaign picture of him in the front window of Lucky Auto and another sign stuck on a stick in our front yard. When the mayor smiles at me, my dad turns and asks me to have a seat over at the counter for a few minutes, and he calls over to Ruth to set me up with a strawberry milkshake. I pick a seat where I'm far enough away from them not to be noticed, but still close enough to hear most of what is being said.

"How's business?"

"No complaints, Mr. Mayor. I expect it will be just the first of many years of prosperity under your many terms in office."

"Good thing you're making some money. I understand you've taken on some additional mouths to feed."

My dad's back is to me, but I can see the mayor's chubby face locked in a stare straight into my dad's eyes.

"A lot of people are talking, Bob, and they aren't too happy with you right now. I know you are a popular guy around here, and I admire your loyalty to an old war buddy, but I think you need to think about yourself right now."

"In other words, you're telling me to let Al go."

"This case can drag on for months, and you are putting yourself needlessly right in the center of the storm. And when it comes to trial, and Kaplan is found guilty, well, believe me, people will forget what a good guy you are and start taking their business elsewhere. I was talking with a couple of the car dealers this morning, and they are just plain shakin' their heads trying to figure out what the hell you're thinking. You know a lot of these guys are pretty close to Chief Wellstone, and he is working overtime getting the word out on Kaplan's arrest."

My dad's head snaps back, almost like he's been punched.

"You know what, Mr. Mayor? You're making a lot of sense. I mean, I've built my business on relationships. Small-town relationships where everybody knows everybody else's business. Giving a job to Al could be a big mistake."

The mayor glances in my direction. "And it's not just about you, Bob. You've got your boy over there to think of. Susan too."

I see my dad turn his head away for the first time as he looks over to me and gives me a big smile, but not his usual smile. This one comes with sad eyes.

"I appreciate the sentiment, I really do. But here's the thing . . . I'm not the only guy with a problem. In fact, you've got a bigger one than I do."

I see the mayor's eyes grow dark and narrow. His smile is frozen on his face now. "Meaning?"

"I know it's barely been two months since you took office, but if a scandal breaks on your watch, you'll take the fall along with the bad guys."

"If you've got something to say to me, then say it."

"Talk to any of your cops. For that matter, talk to damn near anybody on your city payroll. Ask them about how they are treated as employees. Check out the life insurance and the health insurance they help pay for. Check out the retirement plan that they are required to fund."

"I've heard grumbling, but that's what city workers do. They bitch a lot. Hell, I'd like to get paid more, too, but that's not why I took the job."

"You said if I have something to say, then I should just say it. But you're not hearing me. Or maybe you don't want to hear me. It's a small town, Mr. Mayor. Everybody knows that Chief Wellstone runs this place, and everybody knows that his drunk of a brother makes a nice living skimming off the insurance and retirement plans that he has been selling to the city for the past ten years. Aren't you a little curious why the cops pay in so much and have so little to show for it? Well, Al Kaplan wanted to know, and when he started asking around, Ronnie and the chief didn't like it very much, so they told him to back off. And when he told the chief that he'd be looking into policies from other companies, he got hauled out of bed by the chief's buddies over at the sheriff's office, beaten up, and thrown in the slammer. So, like I said, Mr. Mayor, you've got a bigger problem than I do."

I have an ugly vision of Al, now bandaged and limping, being beaten by some men. I visualize Al lying on the ground while crowds of laughing men are kicking and punching him. And then the picture changes, and instead of Al being beaten by the crowd, it's Sammy, and he is calling out to me for help.

The mayor breaks the silence. "They've got a victim with a sworn statement."

"They've probably got a scared kid, a runaway, I hear, whom they can bully into anything. But let's face reality here, Mr. Mayor, when this goes to court, this witness is never going to hold up, and Al will be found not guilty."

"Fine. Then let justice run its course. Just make sure that you get out of the way so that you don't get run over too."

My dad sits in silence for a moment. "Sorry, but no can do. Al's my friend, and I can't let this happen to him. He and his family will be ruined before this ever goes to court. That's what the chief and Ronnie are banking on. That and small-town gossip."

"Well, you're an adult. You pay your taxes, and most importantly, you are a voter, so you can do whatever you damn well please. Just don't say I didn't warn you."

"And don't say I didn't warn you either. But that will be our little secret. I supported you for mayor because I believe you are a good man and you want what's best for this city. And I believe that if you see for yourself that Al has been framed, you'll do the right thing and stand up against the Wellstones, as tough as that will be."

Hearing these men argue, I can't get that picture out of my head of Sammy being beaten, even as I see the mayor get up from the table. Earlier this morning I rode my bike over to Sammy's house so that I could tell him how sorry I was for running away. But when I got there, I was just too embarrassed to knock on the door. So I got back on my bike, and for the second time, I just ran away.

Now, sitting here in the restaurant, my mind keeps going back and forth between two visions. First, I see Al lying on the ground being beaten by some men, then in the blink of an eye, he becomes Sammy. I'm trying to push through the crowd of men to get to Sammy. I want to help him, just like my dad is helping Al. I push and I push and I push.

I hear the sound of breaking glass, too, but I'm surprised when Ruth comes running up to me with a wet towel in her hands. I look down at the ground and see what's left of the tall glass my milkshake had been in, now shattered into small pieces as the splatter of pink liquid on the floor glitters with speckles of glass.

I look up to see the mayor looking over at me, slowly shaking his head in disbelief as he begins to move away from my dad. I notice that neither man extends his hand to the other. The mayor turns once more to my dad.

"Take care of that son of yours, Bob. I'd hate to see anything bad happen to one of my biggest supporters."

They nod at each other, and the mayor walks out the door. When my dad joins me at the lunch counter, I can tell that he's pretty upset. He doesn't even seem to notice Ruth down on her knees, working to clean up my mess.

"Dad, are we going to get in trouble for helping Al?"

"Some people around here think he did a bad thing, and they are pretty upset right now."

"What are we going to do, Dad?"

"What do *you* think we should do?"

I think for a second, think about Sammy too, and then say, "If Al didn't do anything wrong, and he's our friend, then we have to help him out."

"No matter what?"

I smile and nod. "No matter what."

My dad smiles back at me and leans away from the counter. Putting his arm around me, he squeezes my shoulder. "Well, then, that's that. We're agreed. Al stays."

Dad swivels on his stool and helps Ruth stand up, dripping waste pan and all.

"Hey, Ruthie, get us some burgers and fries, pronto. And no flirting with the paying customers. You've got two hungry men over here."

I'm a man? I might as well be. With my dad sitting next to me, I feel about ten feet tall.

"I know the mayor was acting polite and all, but I think he's pretty mad at you."

"I think I straightened him out, son."

"Really?"

"Sure. You just have to know how to talk to people."

10

Fifty-Eight Hours before Sarah's Death

I don't know what Robert said to Bainsworth, but whatever it was, it was good enough to get us moved into a suite about the size of our home back in Potomac.

It only takes us about fifteen minutes to repack our bags and another fifteen minutes to make the escorted walk from the dark side of the Loews tower to the top floor of the Britannia Beach, but like I said about playing craps, what a difference thirty minutes can make.

Our new suite is spectacular, with views of the ocean from every window and a wraparound balcony that we could get lost on.

The main foyer has its own fully stocked bar, and the buffet has been outfitted with mounds of fresh tropical fruit and an enormous platter of hors d'oeuvres, including chilled Bahamian lobsters and gigantic prawns. The seafood is displayed on a mound of ice heaped around an ice carving of a dolphin jumping out of the sea. Jutting out from this sea of ice is a bottle of Dom Perignon champagne with some chilled crystal flutes. A note addressed to "Mr. and Mrs. Josh Brown" is tied around the neck of the bottle with a flurry of ribbons. After popping the cork, I read the note aloud to Sarah, who is sitting on the sofa sipping just enough champagne to share a toast, but with luck, not enough to worsen her ever-present headache:

Dear Mr. and Mrs. Brown,

Welcome to the Britannia Beach Hotel. Please enjoy our hospitality and come back to see us often. Any friend of Robert's is a friend of ours!

Your humble host,
John Bainsworth
Director of VIP Guest Relations
Britannia Beach Hotel

One of the things I have always loved about Sarah is that, like me, she stays on a pretty even keel. Not a lot of highs and lows, just steady. Still, the last twenty-four hours have been beyond anything either of us has ever experienced, and I think we are both in something of a state of shock. I mean, don't get me wrong, when I told Sarah that a single half-hour roll at the crap table had given us $50,000, she was excited. Thunderstruck even, you might say. But I'm not sure that she would have reacted any differently had our take been, say, $5,000, or maybe even $500,000. It is all just Fantasy Land stuff. Out of this world, just like this buffet, which Sarah announces is "such a waste."

"Josh, you're having such a good time with this man, maybe I should just stay up here tonight and let the two of you enjoy yourselves. Besides, my head is killing me."

"Come on, honey, you have to meet him. You have to.

And if your head gets any worse, I'll get up in mid-bite and bring you back up to the suite myself. I promise."

But I can tell there is something else going on here. I press her on it.

"Look, I know that you're not feeling good, I really do, but shit, Sarah, *fifty thousand dollars!* And look at this place. It's just beautiful. This is a once-in-a-lifetime run of good luck, and I'd like to feel just a little more enthusiasm from you. What's the deal here?" The nice little moment we had shared melted with the champagne ice.

"I just miss Richie and Sophie, that's all. And when I called Sherry to give her our new room number, she said that Richie has been coughing, and Sophie won't stop crying."

"Well, I'm sorry, but one of the kids is always coming down with something, and the other one is either throwing a fit or crying, so it's just business as usual. So, I'll ask you again. What's up?"

"Okay, the truth is, this Robert thing is more than a little creepy. I'm just not comfortable with the whole thing. I've never seen you take such an interest in anybody, at least anybody who isn't one of the Redskins, and when you told me that he keeps calling you 'son' and 'my boy,' it all just seems a little too over the top. It's what we talked about this morning down at the pool, but now I think you're actually trying to relive your life with your dad."

"I know how strange it is, but still, I would have thought that you of all people would be happy for me and want to meet him." I toss back a whole flute of the Dom.

"Why *me of all people*? I love you, but I don't believe in ghosts."

"Neither do I." I look Sarah in the eye, hoping that what I'm about to say won't make her headache worse. "You and I both lost our fathers at a young age. You never met my dad, and I never met yours. That's why you have to meet this man. I know that he can't *really* be my father, but he sure seems just like him in every way I remember, so I guess it's the closest you'll ever come to getting to know somebody I loved who died years before we ever even met."

Sarah looks deep into my eyes, almost as if she is trying to read my mind. Taking my hand, she gives me that sad smile and asks, "Why did you want to marry me?"

I smile back. "The bottom line is that when we met, we needed each other. You'd lost both of your parents and I'd lost my dad. I suppose we both had holes in our hearts. . . ." That didn't come out the way I wanted it to. "Like I told Robert this afternoon, we fell in love *because* we needed each other."

A tear starts rolling down her cheek even before I finish talking.

"I *still* need you, Josh. So do Richie and Sophie. But, sometimes, it's like you're just not there with us."

My response catches her off guard. "Do you ever think about what our special, magical connection is?"

She half laughs and half shouts, "What?!"

"What makes the two of us a team? What is it that makes you think about me first thing every morning and last thing every night?"

Sarah just stares back at me, and I'm tempted to reach out and gently close her half-open mouth, but then she speaks.

"I don't know what's come over you, but you're starting

to remind me of that sweet guy that I've always known was buried inside the asshole you've become."

When I try to look hurt, she picks up even more steam. "I don't know who this Robert guy is, but whoever he is, he is clearly having a great influence on you, and I'd like to keep that going. You are happier than I've seen you in a long time. You go on without me, just explain that—"

My soft kiss takes her by surprise and cuts her off mid-sentence. I gently help her to her feet and toward the door in a single motion.

With her free hand, Sarah begins rubbing her fingers across her forehead, a gesture so common these days she probably doesn't even realize she does it any more. She sighs, gives me a sweet smile, and reaches back for her purse on the foyer table by the door.

I'm not sure if I've just been insulted or complimented, and I don't care. I just know that Sarah and Robert have to meet.

———————

Maybe there is a hotter place to be on the island this evening than Café Martinique, but I wouldn't bet on it. Especially not the night before the Super Bowl. The high rollers who came by air, or in many cases on their private yachts, pack the restaurant from end to end.

The room absolutely sparkles. It looks just as I saw it at the theater when James Bond first met the evil Largo and his girlfriend, Domino, in the classic scene from *Thunderball.* Crystal chandeliers, crystal goblets on every table, enormous diamonds on some very lovely (and a few chubby) fingers, and thousands upon thousands of tiny bright lights adorning the yachts in the marina. Every magnificent ship could be admired through the windows lining the back wall of the dining room. Clearly, this is a room filled with people who are used to getting their way, but tonight few if any are more powerful than the maître d', who is literally putting the rich and powerful in their places. Somehow, I'm not surprised to see Robert sitting alone in the center of an enormous banquette set for only three, right in the center of the window seats.

I give Sarah's elbow a gentle squeeze and nod in Robert's direction as we are being led to our position of honor. Through her clenched smile, Sarah whispers, "We obviously don't belong here. Everyone is staring at us." I love it that they are all trying to figure out who we are to rate the best seat in the house.

As we approach the table, Robert slides out of his seat. The smile in my direction is warm but brief. Clearly Sarah is the center of his attention at the moment. Robert takes Sarah's hand in both of his, and then during my brief introductions, to which neither of them pays any attention, he gently puts his arm around Sarah's waist and guides her into the booth. I know by the look she shoots me over her shoulder that Robert might be laying it on just a bit too strong for her taste.

The toasting now begins with more Dom Perignon as Robert praises my afternoon magic with the dice. I can't help thinking this is also the first time somebody is thanking me for getting them money—almost $500,000 in Robert's case. Funny thing too, usually I just hear about people who are pissed off at me, as if it's my fault they're *not* getting any money. Maybe the next time Mr. Scappelli calls, I'll suggest he take up craps!

Through it all, Robert barely takes his smile off Sarah, and after clinking our glasses, he puts his hand on my arm and asks her point-blank, "So, Sarah, what do you think of my boy here?"

"Your boy? I'm sorry, Mr. Saber, but I didn't know that Josh was *your boy*."

Ouch. Robert doesn't even flinch. His smile keeps shining through.

"It's Robert, please. And that's right, I said *my* boy."

"Well, given that you two just met, that's quite a bond. What exactly does it take for somebody to be *your boy*?" Her green eyes flash at Robert, but only in a little playful way.

I wish I could kick Sarah under the table, but the booth is so big I would have had to be a six-and-a-half-foot tight end to reach that far. Robert doesn't seem to be bothered anyway, and he just laughs it off.

"It's simple, Sarah. Anybody who can hold the dice for thirty minutes is *my boy*. In fact, if you come and play some craps with us and hold the dice for that long, you can be one of my boys too!"

Cute. Very cute. Sarah finally laughs and then rolls her eyes at me a little.

Robert takes the liberty of ordering our dinners for us. Caesar salad to start, flaming duck a l'orange for Sarah, and Chateaubriand for two for Robert and me, all to be prepared tableside.

Before the salad can be served, though, our table is visited by a dark shadow in the form of Mr. Bainsworth.

"Good evening, Mr. and Mrs. Brown. I trust that your suite is to your liking and that you enjoyed the simple buffet we arranged. But now, with apologies, I must steal away my good friend Mr. Saber, but just for a moment if you please."

The sweeping motion of his arm is Robert's cue to excuse himself from the table. Most people would be pretty upset to have their dinner interrupted by the staff, but not Robert. He just smiles like it's nothing, and off he goes with Bainsworth.

Alone with Sarah now, I offer, "You know, you could be a little more gracious. Would it kill you?"

"Look, he's a very likable guy. No arguing that. But the whole 'son' and 'boy' routine, it's just so thick."

"So you don't like him after all?"

"Well, I'll give him this, in the first ten minutes he asked a lot of questions about me *and* the kids. It does make me feel like he really wants to know, and he really does care. And he seems particularly concerned about my headaches. I just don't get the whole 'son' thing."

The last part Sarah says under her breath now that Robert is being led back to our table. Bainsworth makes a big production of getting Robert reseated, replacing his napkin, and even refilling the champagne.

Robert returns the kindness, gesturing toward the smiling Brit and saying, "Why thank you, *son*."

Then looking Sarah directly in the eye but grasping Bainsworth's arm, he adds, "I'll tell you what, Sarah, they don't come any better than *my boy* Bainsworth here. Thanks again, Bainsworth. Really. Thank you."

With that slight bow of his, Bainsworth is gone. Sarah's

eyes meet mine along with my unmistakable "I told you so" smirk, which she returns with a smile of her own and a little nod of the head that clearly means "point taken."

In fact, I'd go so far as to say that Sarah not only is no longer feeling creepy about Robert, but over the course of the dinner, she seems to become absolutely enchanted with him. She even seems to enjoy listening to Robert and me talking about tomorrow's Super Bowl. Maybe it's because Robert's Bears aren't playing, but he is doing a good job of including Sarah in the conversation, and she seems to appreciate his cutting me off whenever I get too deep into the teams' stats.

Anyway, it is nice to hear her laughing so much. Better still, over dinner, when Robert asks about her headache, she thinks for a moment and then her surprise clearly shows on her face when she realizes that for the first time in days she is feeling no pain at all.

Over a dessert of crêpes suzette, with tableside service, of course, Sarah changes gears on us both. She asks what she knows I can't. "Robert, I take it that you are here by yourself. Do you have family of your own?"

The smile never leaves his face but the twinkle seems briefly to go out of his eyes.

"Not anymore. I did, though. I had a beautiful wife. You remind me of her in a lot of ways, and together we had a fine son. The kind of son that makes you proud."

Now it is my turn to ask what has been burning me up inside. I barely whisper, "Tell me about him."

Robert looks first to me and then to Sarah with that look of his that goes straight to your heart.

"I can't." That smile. "Sorry, I can't."

Does he mean "can't" as in it's just too painful to discuss? Funny, but I don't think so. Anyway, I'm sure not going to press him on it. Nor is Sarah, who suddenly has tears running down both cheeks. Robert gently puts his hand on the back of her head, and she doesn't resist as he offers her his shoulder. And she thinks Robert and *I* bonded too quickly.

═══════════

We thank Robert for the wonderful meal. My job is to get Sarah safely back up to our suite. Robert's job is to scope out the casino and find the crap table with the best vibes—definitely an art, as any crap player will tell you.

Walking back to the suite, I can tell that Sarah is deep in thought, but when I put my arm around her, she begins to cry. "You were right to make me come to dinner tonight. Your friend is a very special person. A little weird maybe, but special and very kind."

"I knew you'd like him. Who wouldn't? But why are you crying?"

"Because I never knew until tonight how much I missed out on by never knowing your father. And, because I love you, and I feel so bad that someone so special was taken from you, probably when you needed him the most."

"He would have loved you, Sarah." I don't know what else to say.

═══════════

The red message light is flashing as we enter the room. Sarah makes a beeline for the bathroom because her headache came back with a vengeance the minute we left the restaurant. As she walks by, she motions toward the phone.

"Better check it out. Could be Sherry calling about the kids."

And it is Sherry, calling to say that Richie is all better and not to worry. But her message is right after another one, a message from my new buddy Scappelli, whose tone is growing distinctly more hostile with each unwanted call.

I listen to the message, tapping my foot in annoyance. How in the world did this joker get my number?

"Mr. Brown, this is Anthony Scappelli. I got another call with your new room number, so I hope you don't think you can avoid me. I'm sorry it's come to this, but I've hired an attorney in Washington, DC. He will be calling your office on Monday. But I couldn't wait to tell you myself. This lawyer of mine, he's a man who specializes in helping out little guys like me. Little guys who have to take out a second mortgage so that a hospital will admit their daughter when the health insurance plan is unwilling to pay. Good night, Mr. Brown. Although I don't know how someone like you can even sleep at night."

That's just fine. Scappelli's attorney can call any time he wants. My secretary can put him through to any of our own attorneys. He can even take his pick. There are about two dozen to choose from.

"Sarah! Feel better, honey. I'll be back right after Robert and I make another withdrawal from the casino. And don't worry, this time I'll remember to take a key!"

It is nearly midnight, but I grab my Redskins hat and practically run out of the room and down the hall to the elevator. Scappelli can wonder how I sleep at night, but right now I have enough energy to stay up with Robert all night long.

It occurs to me as I ride down to the lobby that I haven't had this much fun since the days of hanging out with my dad.

Can it get any better than this?

11

Four Days before My Father Dies

I t doesn't get any better than this.

Forget what I said about Saturday being my favorite day of the week. It's Sunday. Definitely Sunday. At least during this football season, now that the Bears are one game away from playing the New York Giants for the NFL Championship!

Our game-day ritual is always pretty much the same. My dad makes a big pot of chili, and my mom steams some hot dogs on the stove and broils up some hamburgers in the oven. Then a few minutes before 1:00 p.m., my dad and I grab our plates, head downstairs to the basement, and get all set up in front of the TV. Just the two of us.

My mom has hated football ever since she saw a player get tackled and carried off the field. She's not that thrilled about me watching football on TV either, but she's smart enough to know that's a fight she'll never win with my dad. So most of the time, it's just my dad and me watching the game. But sometimes, like today, Al comes over to join us.

Al's wife and his little kids decide to stay upstairs with Mom. Meanwhile, it takes us three trips to bring down first the chips and other snacks, then the drinks, and then the *real food*. A true football feast.

Our basement is a great place to watch the game. My folks just finished off the main room in knotty pine paneling this past summer. My dad did most of the work down there, with Al helping on some days and James on others, whenever it was slow down at the store. Our TV, a large Magnavox in a beautiful dark wood cabinet, is set up at one end of the room, and at the other end is a bar that my dad also built, with a beautiful neon sign flashing *Drink Pabst Blue Ribbon Beer*. When it comes time to watch TV, I always sit on the sofa, and my dad plops down in his new Barcalounger recliner, custom ordered in Bears' orange-and-blue Naugahyde vinyl.

Today is the first time Al has seen my dad's new recliner, and he doesn't need much encouragement to try it out. He sits down and immediately tries to push the seat back, but it won't budge.

My dad smirks. "Oh, I'm sorry. Operating these chairs requires a certain minimum level of intelligence. Let me help you."

With that, my dad pushes down on the control lever that's just out of Al's sight, and the chair snaps back so hard that Al lets out a giant yell as his ankles shoot well above his head. My mom calls down to make sure everything is okay, but I guess when she hears my dad and me howling, she figures it out for herself.

Meanwhile, Al's just sitting there with his head back and his feet up, with his pant legs falling down almost to his knees. I don't know which of us sees it first, but right there in plain view is a small pistol in a holster strapped to Al's now-bare ankle.

My dad just about screams, but then hushes himself, "A

gun! A gun? Are you kidding me, Al? You're out on bail, for God's sake. What the hell are you doing with a gun?"

By this point Al has figured out where the lever is, so he manages to put the chair back in its upright position and get a little dignity back.

"What do you think I'm doing with a gun? What do you think? Jesus Christ, they broke down my door! Who knows what they'll try next."

A strange silence hangs in the air. Finally my dad just nods, saying, "Okay, Al." Then he walks slowly over to the TV to turn up the volume. I think if I weren't in the room, things might have been different, but both my dad and Al are content to drop it for the moment and move on to football.

And what football this is going to be: the most important game I have ever seen. Yesterday, the New York Giants beat Philadelphia 21 to 7 in Philadelphia, so the regular season ended with the Giants winning the Eastern Conference. The Western Conference, on the other hand, is all coming down to today's game. The Lions' record is 9 and 2, just besting the Bears' record of 8 and 2 plus one tie—and that tie came in an earlier game against the Giants, of all teams.

The Lions, with Pro-Bowler Bobby Layne at quarterback, are a big favorite coming into the game, especially since they killed the Bears 42-10 in their last match-up just a few weeks ago. My dad almost throws his hot dog at Al when he says, "The smart money has got to be all over Detroit."

At 1:00 p.m. sharp, my dad, Al, and I all stand up and put our hands over our hearts as the national anthem plays. At 1:05 p.m. I stand up again—jump up, actually—for the kick-off in front of a packed house at Wrigley Field.

At the first commercial break, my dad hands me his and Al's empty beer bottles and asks me to grab them each a cold one from the small refrigerator behind the bar. As I walk over, Dad asks Al, "So how did it go yesterday with your first day of honest work?"

Al kind of shrugs. Under his breath he mutters, "It was okay, I guess."

Never one to let things alone, my dad comes right back at him.

"That's it? Just okay?"

"Okay, Bob. Fine. I'll say it: James is a good guy. Like I said, it went fine. Happy now?"

My dad just smiles and yells over to ask where I am with their beers.

For the rest of the afternoon I bring Al and Dad fresh beers whenever they are ready. That's my job. Ed Brown, the Bears' Pro-Bowl quarterback, has the job of getting points on the scoreboard, while J. C. Caroline and the rest of the Bears' defense has the job of shutting down Detroit.

We all do our jobs just fine.

Final score: Chicago Bears 38. Detroit Lions 21.

The NFL Championship match-up for the 1956 season is set for Sunday, December 30, 1956. New York Giants move over. The Bears are coming to town!

———

By 5:00 p.m. the Kaplans are long gone, but my dad and I are both still sky high with excitement. Dad insists that we go out to celebrate the big victory. So we all wash up, change clothes, and head over to Tiebel's Restaurant in

Schererville for the best dinner in town. They're known for their fried chicken, perch filets, and sautéed frog legs. Dad says that a lot of Chicago people think they're pretty smart for knowing about Phil Schmidt's in Hammond, but only the smartest know enough to drive a little farther and go to Tiebel's instead. Best of all, Mom says I have enough time to get a dish of butter pecan ice cream and we can still get home before *The Ed Sullivan Show* starts.

On the way home Dad gives Mom that great crazy smile of his, a surefire tip-off that something is coming. Mom watches dad grab the heater control on the dashboard and turn it up as far as it can go. Knowing what's coming next, she pleads, "Oh no, Bob. Please, no."

It is barely above zero outside, but my dad starts rolling down his window, and he yells for Mom and me to do the same.

"Windows down, everybody!"

"Come on, Mom, windows down."

Mom just shrugs and rolls her window down too, complaining that she's shut in the car with two lunatics. Once her window is all the way down, Dad says, "Okay, everyone, on the count of three. One, two, three."

So, barreling along on a frigid December night with our windows wide open, we start singing at the top of our lungs:

Bear down, Chicago Bears, make every play, clear the way to victory;

Bear down, Chicago Bears, put up a fight with a might so fearlessly.

We'll never forget the way you thrilled the nation,
with your T-formation.

Bear down, Chicago Bears, and let them know why you're wearing
the crown.
You're the pride and joy of Illinois,
Chicago Bears, bear down!

—————

As we are driving up to our home, Mom points through the windshield at the house.

"There's a car out front. I think it's Roberta Johnson."

I know right away that she's right. The car is an old Plymouth, dented more places than not, the rear bumper hanging on by some tape. The motor is still running, and the dome light is on inside the car. My dad pulls up right behind them and gives a friendly little toot on the horn.

Mom turns to Dad, saying, "You know, I can't remember the last time I saw Roberta. I hope everything is all right."

But I know better. I'm sure I'm going to be sick.

Mom and Dad hop quickly out of the car, but I'm moving a lot slower, hanging back. I can see, though, that Mrs. Johnson is yelling at Sammy, who is also refusing to get out of the car. He's just sitting there in the front seat with his arms folded over his chest, staring straight ahead.

My mom walks right to Mrs. Johnson's side.

"Roberta? What is it, love? What's the matter?"

Mrs. Johnson had parked the car directly under a bright streetlight, and I could see that her eyes were all red and puffy. I always remember Mrs. Johnson the way she was when Sammy and I started kindergarten together and they lived next door. Since Mom was working at the store, I would go to the Johnsons' house every day after school. She would make Sammy and me lunch, and then we'd go up to his room and play all afternoon, or maybe on a nice day we'd go outside and play tag or something. Every afternoon when Beth would get home from school, Mrs. Johnson would call us back into the kitchen and give us all a snack. My favorite was fresh sliced apples smeared with peanut butter. I spent so much time at their home, it started to feel like my own, and I always looked forward to seeing Mrs. Johnson after school. She looked so pretty all the time. I especially liked how Sammy would try to squirm away from her and yell when she'd give him a big hug and kiss. I always got a quick hug, too, and it made me feel nice and warm.

It's been about three years now since Sammy's dad left and they had to move. I can't believe how much she's changed. In place of her nice clothes are some baggy slacks and a torn housecoat, and her hair looks kind of dirty and stringy. Except for the red rings around her eyes, her face looks pale, like maybe she's sick or something.

Mrs. Johnson yells into her car through the open driver's side door, "Sammy, get out! Get out of the car right this minute so that your good friends can see you."

Sammy gives one quick "no!" and continues staring straight out the windshield.

Mom glances at Dad and softly says his name.

Mrs. Johnson keeps screaming for Sammy to get out of the car, and she's crying pretty hard now. Mom holds her as Dad walks over to the car.

"Okay if I join you, Sammy?" There is no response, but Dad gently sits down next to Sammy anyway and closes the door. I can't hear what, if anything, they're saying, but I can see my father touching Sammy's face and turning his head to get a better look. After a few minutes Dad gets back out of the car and rejoins the women, but his eyes are boring right into me.

"Sammy's pretty banged up. Two black eyes, a couple of broken teeth, and some nasty cuts and bruises." Dad sighs.

Mrs. Johnson is still crying. She tells Mom and Dad that Sammy is always coming home hurt, but never this bad before. I can feel my dad's eyes burning right into me as he walks over and firmly leads me away from the others.

"Sammy says that he fell off his bike on his way home from playing with you after school on Thursday. Mrs. Johnson has kept him home since then and told him he wasn't allowed out of his room until he would tell her what really happened. After three days of getting nowhere, she made Sammy get into the car and come over here. Now why, Josh, do you suppose Mrs. Johnson would do that?"

I'm hanging my head because I can't look my dad in the eye. I just whisper, "I don't know."

"Do you want to tell me what happened to Sammy?"

"I guess he fell off his bike. Lots of kids do." I keep looking at my feet.

Silence. Just silence for what seems like forever. I don't lift my head up, but after a while I hear his shoes making a soft crunching sound as he walks away across the icy ground. He doesn't even bother to tell me he knows I'm lying. He just walks away. I feel ashamed, but even more than that I feel trapped. If I tell my dad the truth, that I ran away from my best friend when he was being beaten up and needed me the most, well, who could be proud of a son like that?

Dad tells Mrs. Johnson that he'll call later if he finds out anything—anything he can believe. My mom urges Mrs. Johnson to come into the house for some tea, but she refuses.

Mom asks, "Roberta, have you had any word from Beth?"

Mrs. Johnson looks so sad. She shakes her head shakes and raises her hands to the sky.

"Three months now, not a word. I don't even know if she's alive. Beth blames me for her father leaving. It's been hard, really hard. She's still only seventeen, but she took up with some punk in his twenties who has a police record. When I wouldn't let them come into the house, she just took off. Ran away without even a note."

My dad jumps right in. "Roberta, if you hear from Beth, you have to call me. Okay? It's important, Roberta. Call me right away."

"Sure. Whatever you say."

My mom gives her a hug and then walks over to stand close to my father as we watch Mrs. Johnson get back into her car and slowly drive off. Mom tells Dad she had no idea things had gotten so bad for her.

I can't think of too many times when I've seen my Dad really angry, but today is sure one of them. He is angry about what happened to Sammy for sure, but I think even more he is disappointed, sad even. He looks right at me and says, "I need you to go up to your room right now. You and I will talk later."

―――――――

Even though it's still early, I put my pajamas on and climb into bed. In my mind I keep seeing Sammy and me both lying on the cold ground and that sad look of his when Mickey and the others started beating up on him. He didn't ask me for help. He just looked right at me. He didn't even call for me to stop when I got to my feet and started running away just as fast as I could.

I'm trying to fall asleep, but every time I close my eyes, there's Sammy. He is lying on the ground getting punched and kicked, and then I see him sitting in his mom's car with my dad talking to him. And then I see my dad's face with that look of complete disappointment, and I want to die.

I close my eyes and bury my face in the pillow. I'm not sure how long I lie there like that, but after a while I feel the bed move, and I roll over to see my dad sitting on the edge. He is right where he was a few nights before when I told him that Sammy and I both ran away from those kids. Now he knows the truth.

"Hi, Dad."

"Josh, I need to ask you a question. Would you ever steal?"

"No, honest. I could never steal anything."

"Well, you know what? Lying is the same as stealing. When somebody lies, they're stealing the truth. It's just like stealing something out of a store, only maybe even worse. You don't steal. You don't cheat. And you don't lie. It's not who we are. It's not who *you* are, Josh. *You're my boy,* and I just know it. It's not who you are."

My dad stands up and looks down at me lying in my bed.

"You let me know when you want to tell me the truth. No reason to talk until then."

Dad turns to leave, and over his shoulder he gives a sad wave. "Good night, son."

He's halfway to my door when I sit up with a jolt and scream at him through the tears, which come out of nowhere.

"I was scared! Don't you know that? I was so scared!"

He turns and comes back to the side of my bed.

"Scared? I remember you told me you were scared the night that it happened. I sat right on this bed and you told me that Mickey Wellstone and his friends were teasing you and Sammy, and you said the two of you ran away. Is that the scared you're talking about?"

"I got knocked down by Mickey, and Sammy came to help me. Then they all turned on Sammy. He was on the ground, and those guys were all kicking and punching him. I could have helped him, but I was scared and I ran away. I haven't called Sammy since it happened. He must hate me. *You* must hate me."

Dad sits down on the bed again, but he's silent for the longest time. Finally he asks, "What do you want to do now?"

"Well, I know one thing. I can't go on that school trip. Those guys will beat the crap out of me. Sammy can't go because he said his mom doesn't have the money. He probably wouldn't want to be with me any more anyway. And I can't go because I'll get killed."

"Listen to me, Josh. You're going on that trip. Sammy's going too, because I'll pay for it."

"But what about Mickey?"

"You are going to have to deal with bullies for the rest of your life. They're everywhere. Sometimes they'll come after you, and sometimes you'll see them go after somebody else, but there will always be bullies. But I'll tell you what there may *not* always be. There may not always be a good friend around like Sammy. So when you have a friend, a real friend, you treasure him. You don't let him go, and you don't let anything happen to him, not if you can help it anyway. And that's where you'll get your strength from."

"I'm still scared, Dad. I'll go because you want me to, but I'm still scared."

"That's okay. It's okay to be scared. But remember, you've got something else going for you."

"What?"

"Me. I'll always be there for you. You've got me."

12

Fifty-Three Hours before Sarah's Death

The call from Scappelli is more of a nuisance than anything else. So he's hired a D.C. attorney, big deal. At Grand National, lawsuits are just part of our cost of doing business, and it's all built into our business modeling. He doesn't scare me. Few people do. Still, I guess I don't blame him for trying. It's gotta be tough seeing your own kid sick.

The moment the elevator opens on the lobby level, I'm hit with a blast of noise from the throng of partygoers who seem to be everywhere. The excitement in the air is palpable. It's nearly midnight, and my first thought is that Sarah must be the only guest who is already in bed. The resort is just bursting with energy. People are laughing and drinking, there are cigars everywhere, and a lot of the women are dressed to the nines. And then, of course, there are the yachters, easily spotted in their white captain's hats and blazers.

I head straight for the casino along a now-familiar path that takes me past a couple of top-drawer jewelry stores. Hmm, maybe I should go into one later and pick up something nice for myself. Diamond cufflinks seem appropriate . . . or, I don't know, maybe I should get something for Sarah and my mom. I wonder if they'd like that?

The crowds in the lobby are just a sneak preview of what is around the corner. The casino itself is packed from end to end so that even walking through it is difficult. I'm guessing it takes me a good ten minutes just to get to the crap tables. There are five tables in all, arranged like a gigantic capital U, creating a large central pit for the bosses and other staffers. Four of the tables are maxed out at sixteen players each, but with friends, onlookers, and eager gamblers waiting for an open slot, there must be more than fifty people crowded around each of the four busiest tables.

The fifth table, the one at the base of the U, is practically empty, except for a smiling Robert and a few glum losers. That's the thing about craps: most players are superstitious, and they'd rather stand around waiting for an open spot at a hot table than walk right up to the half-empty table right next door where the dice are clearly cold. Mathematically, of course, cold dice are no predictor of what the future will hold. Each of the possible numbers between two and twelve has its own exact odds of coming up, but don't try to tell that to a veteran shooter. Some tables are hot, some are cold, and that's that.

I walk up to Robert's right side, the same side where I stood during this afternoon's triumph, and we both flash gigantic smiles like two kids about to see Santa.

"You sure this is the right table? Everybody else seems to think the action is everywhere but here."

Before he can answer, the pit boss walks up to us holding a clipboard in one hand and a gold pen in the other. "Good evening, Mr. Saber, Mr. Brown. Can I arrange for your markers?"

Robert signs for $100,000, and I take $5,000, leaving me nearly $45,000 in my casino account. God only knows what Robert has in his account. No sooner do Robert and I get our chips than our table starts to fill up with players who remember me from my great roll this morning. I guess when you've held the dice for almost half an hour, you become a casino celebrity in some circles. My fan club is returning.

Robert breaks the silence while we wait for our chips. "Nice crowd, huh? Pretty much like last night's, I'd say."

Robert and I haven't talked much about what we each do for a living. I know that he's a consultant of some kind, and he knows that I'm an exec with Grand National, but I don't want to brag and tell him that I'm considered an expert on identifying groups of people. Still, I can't resist trying to impress him a little now; maybe I want to make him like me even more. "No, I'd say this crowd is different from last night's. Big difference, in fact."

Robert smiles and seems surprised. "Really? I look around and I still see some very rich guys smiling and laughing. Some beautiful ladies too, out on the town and enjoying every minute of it. Not much difference from yesterday that I can tell."

I can't help but smile back. "Look at the colors," I say, gesturing around the casino. Everywhere we look we see the Dolphins' orange and turquoise, or the burgundy and gold of my Skins. "These colors tell a story, Robert, but it's a very different one from last night. Do you see it?"

Robert looks bored and shrugs his shoulders. "The colors just tell me that there is no justice and I'm the only guy here wearing a Chicago hat. The colors tell me that the

Bears have to wait one more year to play in the Super Bowl. The colors tell me that the best is yet to come!"

I laugh and begin to explain what's different about this group of fans. I'm trying hard to sound like an expert, not just an out-and-out braggart.

"Not quite what I had in mind. Yesterday, I figured the crowd to be about fifty-fifty, but today clearly the Dolphins' colors easily outnumber the gold and burgundy of Redskins fans. Now why would that be?"

"Well, Josh, I'm sorry to say it, but the Dolphins are big favorites to win. Looks to me like a lot of your Redskins fans have crossed over to the other side."

"Very funny, but no. The first possibility is that it is past midnight and that Redskins fans as a group go to bed earlier than Dolphins fans. You buy that one?

"Sure. Could be."

"Actually not. You see, the Washington, D.C., market is a much younger one than Miami, and there is a direct correlation between age and how early you go to bed. If anything, based on that theory, there should be more Skins fans here right now."

More and more players are coming to our table now, and the stickman is holding back the dice while the newcomers get set up. So I continue.

"Now, it's also possible that the large Latin population in Miami has a strong desire to associate with an American icon like a sports team, so they disproportionately wear their colors relative to non-Hispanic segments."

Robert rolls his eyes and in the flattest possible monotone whispers, "Fascinating." Okay, he's bored silly. I'd better wrap this up before I lose him for good.

"No, the Hispanic thing is interesting, but I'd say that in this case, simple geography takes the trump. This crowd has gone from fifty-fifty to seventy-thirty in one day because the Miami crowd doesn't mind coming down for just two days. Hell, it's only a forty-minute flight, so they started to show up en masse this morning. Interesting group behavior, but pretty simple actually."

"Josh, let me get this straight. When you look around, you don't see people? Only groups?"

Well, at least he understands what I'm saying.

"Sure, but in this case, it's not the demographics and it's not the cultural psychographics. It's just simple geography that has driven this change. Pretty interesting stuff, wouldn't you say?"

I'm pretty proud of myself right now even if Robert doesn't care.

The stickman has been busy with the new arrivals, and I now have my five thousand in front of me right next to Robert's hundred grand. The rest of the players have already placed their bets so I put five hundred on the line next to Robert's ten thousand. Yes, ten thousand! The night is about to get under way.

I start to reach for the dice, but Robert stops my hand with a firm grip on my wrist. He looks troubled, and now *his* arm sweeps the casino crowd.

"Let me ask you a question. Do you know any of the people in here?"

I shrug. "Not that I know of, why?"

"It's just sort of sad, that's all. I look around, and I see people. Some are happy, and some are scared. There are old and young. There are pretty and plain and everything in between. But you're not seeing them. You're just seeing groups."

The stickman, who has been waiting patiently in deference to Robert's VIP status, finally succumbs to a few of the players on the other side of the table who are clamoring for my first roll.

Still troubled by Robert's comment, I sweep the dice off the green felt and let them fly hard against the mirror at the other side of the table.

"Loser 3. Craps 3. Line away and pay the Don'ts."

Shit! Five hundred gone on the first roll. Robert's ten grand disappears too. He replaces his loss with another ten thousand without even blinking. I throw down a single pink five-hundred-dollar chip and grab the dice once more. I'm about to throw again, but Robert's comment rankles, and I can't wait any longer to clear the air.

"Hey, do you think I'm some kind of bad guy? This is what I do. This is why the big boys at Grand National love me. Anybody can see people. I see groups, and I see how they act, and I do it well."

Then the stickman interrupts again with, "Excuse me, sir, but the dice . . . *please.*"

I let 'em fly. Angry dice bouncing once more off the wall.

"Loser 2. Loser. Take the line."

Shit! That was a quick thousand.

I feel Robert's eyes drilling right into me as he turns to the pit boss with an unusual request.

"We'd like to pass the dice and take a quick break."

"Of course, Mr. Saber. At your convenience."

The pit boss motions for a security guard to protect our place at the table while we're gone. I suppose if you're a big enough gambler, you can probably get away with just about anything you want.

Robert says, "Just leave your chips on the table. They'll be fine while we're gone."

———

He leads me back into the private VIP lounge, unmindful of the chorus of groans from the players we're leaving behind. Most of them joined our table hoping for a repeat of my earlier success, and now they're all losing and having to fend for themselves and hoping that we'll get back soon. And this time, with a hotter hand.

We walk to the back of the lounge and I settle into a rich, soft black leather chair. Though I'm not looking at him, I can feel Robert's eyes boring into me. I wave off the approaching cocktail waitress, and apparently so does Robert, as we sit alone in silence for several minutes.

That this man, this incredible man, is clearly upset with me scares me speechless. I can only guess that everything I'm doing now is putting a wedge between us, driving him away after he came so blessedly into my life.

Twenty minutes ago, when I walked into the casino, I could feel the warmth of Robert's glow. Twenty minutes ago, I felt like my father was back in my life. Now, sitting here next to him, afraid to look at him, I can feel his disappointment. I can feel him slipping away from me.

A stranger walking by would have thought I was sleeping in that deep chair—passed out, more like it, from a little too much of the good life. Hardly. My mind is racing, and deep within me I feel an ache, an emptiness coming maybe from the pit of my stomach—or maybe it's my heart.

My cockiness is gone, my confidence behind me. I can't even speak for fear of saying the wrong thing again and losing him forever. Does he hate me now? Have I hurt him? After all this, I'm so close. Have I let him down?

When he puts his hand on my arm, I cringe, as if every muscle in my body is clenching and trying to pull away from whatever is coming next. And then I slowly realize that his touch, the touch that had electrified me and warmed me whenever he shook my hand or gave me a friendly hug, had turned to ice.

Then almost a whisper. "Josh?"

I open my eyes and slowly turn my head, and I feel like I'm going to be sick. It's still Robert sitting beside me, but barely. His deep tan has been replaced by a pale, almost blue pallor; his meticulously groomed hair seems lifeless and disheveled. But what shocks me more than anything else are his eyes, still deep and dark, but now without that sparkle. His smiling eyes are gone, leaving only sadness in their place. I have a crazy thought that somehow I'm killing him.

He pleads with me, "They are people, Josh, *people.* You're telling me that you don't even see them?"

I want so much to please this man, to have him like me. I want—no, I need—him to be proud of me. As I look into his sad eyes, I *know* this soul is precious. Something precious, to be kept close, to be studied and adored, to be drunk from. But I know, I know I've broken his heart, and his sadness washes over me.

"I'm sorry."

"Sorry for what? Sorry for bringing an old man back down to earth?"

Have I brought him back down to earth?

"No. I'm sorry because I think you are seeing me for who I am, seeing the man I've become, and it's not who you want me to be."

Robert remains deep in thought for quite a while. Finally he speaks.

"Will you do something for me?"

I slowly nod. I don't think there's anything I won't do for him. Or at least try to do.

"Will you come back to the casino with me and look at those people in there? I mean *really look* at them. For the first time in a long, long time I want you to really *see* them. Try to feel their presence, their happiness, their concerns, their wants and needs. Feel their life."

My hand falls from my head onto my leg with a dull thump.

"That's not who I am, and it's not what I do. I stand back from people, and I study them. Then I put them in their proper groups and figure out what they are going to do, how they will behave. That's just what I do."

"But you can't touch them, right? And you can't let their lives touch yours. Maybe not even your own kids? Maybe not even Sarah?"

I try to sit up a little straighter in my chair. "I'm doing okay." Hearing my voice, even I don't believe my own words. But when he begins to talk, I look once more into his eyes.

"You were hurt, Josh. Someone who loved you very much hurt you. I know he didn't mean to. I know he told you he'd never leave you, but he did. Not his fault, but gone is gone, right?"

I sit back and close my eyes again, this time to try and hold back the tears.

"He doesn't have to be gone," Robert whispers, gently tapping my chest. "He can stay right here. Let him in, Josh. Just let him in."

We sit in silence once more as I try desperately to sort out what is happening. What does this all mean? What are the stakes here? And the biggest question of all escapes my lips.

"Robert, are you my father?"

I open my eyes to see his response. That smile. So kind.

"Do you want me to be?"

I close my eyes one more time. The thought of losing him, again, is more than I can stand. Whatever it takes, I can't let him out of my life now. I turn to face him once more and am pleased to see the color returning to his skin.

"You're saying you want to *teach* me to care about people?"

"No. You were taught that a long, long time ago. I just want you to remember how."

My throat is so dry I'm barely able to speak. I'm not sure he can even hear me when I ask him, "What do you want me to do?"

"Not much, really. Just come back over to that crap table with me. You know, it's a great place to look at people. Just look around you and soak it all in. Soak *them* in. Make a connection. They're *people,* Josh. Some good and some bad, but they share this place with you, and they all need you. And *you* need them."

Robert takes my arm, the warmth now back in his touch; firmly pulling me to my feet, he puts his arm around me and guides me back to the table one more time.

"Come on, son. Let's have ourselves some fun!"

━━━━━━━━

"Hey look, they're back! About time, for Christ's sake. We're getting killed here!"

I look over at the man who is so pleased to see us that he announces it to the whole table. He has the dice in front of him, so he is also the shooter.

He is an older man, I'd say at least in his seventies, but he has a nice smile, with bright sparkly eyes that make him look more like a kid.

"Where've you been, guys? We've been dying over here without you!"

I looked to Robert and, like our new friend at the other end of the table, he is beaming. I look back across the way to the shooter, and from twenty feet away I can feel, yeah, actually *feel* him reaching me.

He points a sharp finger at me from the far side of the table. "That guy's the shooter. Let's all pass him the dice."

I can feel everyone at the table looking at me, looking to me for another repeat performance, like I could somehow control the dice. Others add their voices as well. "Come on. Pass him the dice!"

"No sir." I say, pointing back at my new friend across the table. "*You're* the shooter. We're all shooters! Now let's have some fun!"

With a shrug of his shoulders and one more smile, he sweeps the dice into his hand. All the while, he keeps his eyes locked on mine.

"Get a big bet down there, sonny. Your Uncle Irv is going to roll, and I'm about to kick some butt!"

So he rolls.

And he rolls.

And he rolls.

When the seven finally comes out six passes later, our shooter raises his locked hands above his head, proclaiming himself victorious to the cheers of the crowd.

The dice are passed to a beautiful black woman in her late forties. She introduces herself to the table as Millie and says for all to hear, "Uncle Irv here is going to bless these blessed dice. Come on, dice; be nice to these fine people." And they are.

After Millie comes Ralph, who is on his honeymoon with Margie. She stays right on his side with her hand on his neck the whole time he rolls—about fifteen minutes' worth. Now that's love. And more applause.

Then it's Connie and Katie's turn. Twin sisters. One in Redskin's colors, and one favoring the Dolphins. Shit, now I've seen it all. Connie is good to us too. Katie is even better. And that from a Miami fan!

All in all, it takes nearly two hours for the dice to get to my end of the table and finally passed to me. The stickman has set them up with a 6 and a 5 showing. I guess the casino is keeping its sense of humor despite all the money they've forked over.

My rack is full. The outside tier is jet black; $100 chips from end to end. The inner tier tells the story though, split pretty evenly between the purple $500s and the even prettier chips that are worth $2,500 each.

Funny thing about craps. Winning can drain you as much as losing. I look down at all those chips, then to the dice, and then to see Robert nodding at me, letting me know without even saying it that my next move is the right one. Dozens of smiling faces look over to me from every direction.

In my loudest voice, I say, "I want to thank you all, my friends. Thank you for this beautiful evening. I'm going to pass on these dice because I can't do any better than any of you. I'll say goodnight to you all now, and remember, everyone, ALL HAIL TO THE REDSKINS!"

I pump my fist into the sky amid a pretty even mix of cheers and boos. Robert waves goodnight to the crowd, and security scoops up our chips for the short walk over to the private VIP cashiers.

What great people these were! We laughed, we joked, we yelled and screamed, and best of all, we killed the house. When I'm all cashed in, and over $150,000 has been deposited into my casino account, I've probably won more than most everyone at the table. Everyone, that is, except for Robert. The people at the table would tell the story for years to come. It's not very often that you get to see someone win over a million dollars.

———

Tomorrow would be my day, maybe the best day in my life. Start the morning golfing with Robert, and then bring Sarah up to his suite to watch my Skins in the Super Bowl.

And finally, tuck Sarah into bed and kill the casino one more time.

We get into an empty elevator. "I won't ever forget tonight."

"We met some pretty friendly dice tonight, didn't we?" Robert says.

"Actually, I was thinking more about Irv."

I'm enjoying playing the whole scene over in my head.

"Irv and Millie, Ralph and Connie and Katie. The whole lot of them. What a crew!"

That smile. It's like his heart is coming right out of his being. And I smile right back.

I've made him proud.

"Do you have many friends, Josh? Did you ever?"

Hands in my pockets, I look down at my feet as the picture in my mind turns to Sammy. Sammy, lying on the ground and looking so sad.

"Once. But we've kind of grown apart."

"I'll bet he was a good friend to you."

I see that the toe of my left shoe is all scuffed, probably from kicking the base of the crap table. Without even looking up, I know that Robert is staring at me.

"He was the best. The best friend I'll ever have."

"Well, at least that's an honest answer."

"You know that you never answered *my* question."

Robert smiles and puts his hand on my shoulder.

"Right. You want to know if I'm your father who passed away twenty-five years ago. How much did you have to drink tonight anyway? Get some sleep. We're golfing tomorrow and I have every intention of taking away some of that cash you earned today."

That's okay. I couldn't be more contented then I am right now. This whole day has been incredible, and I'll leave it at that.

"Good night, Robert."

"Good night, son."

―――――――

I'm so focused on being quiet as I slip into bed, that I don't even see the note that Sarah has left on my pillow until I roll over face first right into it. I tiptoe over to the window and pull the drapes aside just a crack so that I can read her handwriting in the moonlight.

Phil called around 11pm. He said to tell you not to bother calling him back. I'm pretty sure he was drunk, and he really sounded pissed off!
Love,
me

Not what I planned on thinking about as I drift off to sleep. . . .

13

Two Days before My Father Dies

A lot of families have traditions during the holidays, but not too many kids in Hammond, Indiana, spend every Christmas on the local golf course, which as often as not is covered with snow and ice this time of year. As far as I can see, that tradition belongs to just my dad and me.

Even Mom has given up arguing about us going out in the dead of winter. Well, almost given up. As she gives us each a thermos of hot soup, she says, "Bob, I don't know why you boys even bother. Those jackets are so big and clumsy; you can't possibly swing a golf club."

"Don't worry honey," my dad says as we walk out the door. "We'll leave the coats in the car like we always do."

"BOB BROWN, YOU WILL NOT!"

My dad and I can't even keep a straight face. "Just kidding, Sue. We'll be back in four hours. Tops."

Dad has already put the clubs in the back of the car, and we head off down Hohman Avenue to the course at Northwest Park. This Christmas is shaping up perfectly, too. Blue skies, temperatures in the balmy thirties, and beautiful wet white snowflakes falling at a pretty good clip. Snowflakes that are wet enough for packing snowballs and pretty just the same.

As we drive along, Dad reviews some golf swing basics.

"Remember, Josh, that little ball only weighs about two ounces, even covered in bright red paint like ours. You don't have to try and kill it. Just make a nice smooth pass at it, and more than anything else—"

"I know, Dad, *keep my eye on the ball.*"

"No, mister wisenheimer. That's not what I was going to say. Always remember, more than anything else, to pick a target. Don't think about anything else. Just get that picture in your head and hit the ball right at your target. Target, target, *target.* Got it?"

"Got it, Dad. Pick a—"

The police siren cuts me off mid-sentence. My dad's eyes shoot up to the rear-view mirror.

"Jesus Christ. Are you kidding me?"

"Were we speeding, Dad?"

"Speeding? I'm doing a slick twenty-five miles an hour in this snow. No, this joker is probably mad because I haven't put chains on my tires. Like I'm going to get stuck or something."

Dad stares straight ahead, and I can tell he's pretty mad. He doesn't even bother to turn around, but when he hears the ice crunching under the policeman's feet, he starts to roll down the window.

"Merry Christmas, Bob." Then in my direction. "Merry Christmas there, young man."

My dad's head snaps around to the face that is now practically stuck inside our car.

"Merry Christmas to you, Chief. What's the deal? Are you trying to save on staff overtime by working the streets yourself?"

Chief Wellstone laughs, but even I can tell it isn't a real laugh, any more than my dad sounded like he meant it when he wished the chief a Merry Christmas.

The chief motions toward the backseat with a thumb gloved in shiny black leather. "Mind if I jump in for a minute?"

"Well, I'm not getting out, so help yourself." Dad's voice is as icy as the road.

The chief reaches through my dad's open window and unlocks the back door. A moment later, he's sitting in back, but my dad won't even turn around to face him. He just stares at him through the mirror.

"So you pulled us over to wish us a Merry Christmas? That's pretty Christian of you, Chief."

The chief chuckles.

"Why, thanks, Bob. We've got a lot of good Christians around here, you know. Fine people. Fine town. Christian town. Know what I mean, Bob?"

"Well, let's see. Could this have anything to do with my getting Al Kaplan out of the Crown Point slammer and giving him a job? Am I getting warm here, Chief?"

My dad might not want to be looking over his shoulder, but I'm not going to miss this. I'm on my knees turned all the way around, and I can tell that even though the chief has a big smile on his face, he is mad. Real mad.

"Look, I've told you before: you've got a lot of friends in this town, but you're making a lot of enemies too. What happened to that little girl was a crime, and he's going to pay."

"I don't think so, and neither do you. The only thing Al did wrong was figure out that your brother has been screwing over your own officers. Why don't you try doing something worthwhile like finding Roberta Johnson's daughter instead of throwing an honest cop into a filthy cell?"

A silence hangs over us all. The chief isn't even pretending to smile anymore.

"You know that the victim has identified him. Positive ID, right out of the lineup. I don't know how it happened, but the word on your buddy has gotten out all over town. People are pretty mad, and they are starting to get mad at you, too."

"I want to thank you for pulling me over just to wish Josh and me a Merry Christmas, Chief."

"I pulled you over to warn you. People are mad, and sometimes angry people do stupid things."

The smile returns to the chief's face as he leans forward and gives my head a friendly little shake.

"Angry people do stupid things, Bob. You've got a son here to think of. Wife too. I can't be everywhere at once to protect you, either. That's all I'm saying. People are mad as hell."

For the first time my dad takes his eyes away from the rearview mirror, and his whole body snaps around. The chief pulls back, and for a moment his eyes grow wide with fear.

"Is that a threat, Wellstone? Is that what this is all about? Do you really think you and your idiot brother can scare me?"

Their eyes lock, faces only inches apart. Finally, the chief moves his gaze to the seat next to him, where our golf clubs sit.

"Headed out to Northwest Park, boys? Nice place for

a little winter golf. Nice all year-round in fact, especially since there are no Jews or coloreds out there. Have a good game, Brown. And take good care of that boy of yours."

My dad doesn't even bother to answer; he just slowly turns around and stares out the front windshield. The chief lets out a heavy sigh and sits very still, as if trying to figure out what to do next.

I continue to stare into the chief's face, but all I can see is Al and Sammy, doubled over on the ground, beaten and bruised.

The scream is so loud that it takes us all by surprise, even me, and it's my own voice. "Police are supposed to be the good guys. You're just a bad man. You're just a BAD MAN!"

My dad's looking at me in total disbelief. But I'll never forget the chief's cold, hard stare. His eyes never leave my face, even as he quietly gets out of our car.

Other than the thud of the slamming door, silence hangs in the air, and I don't know what to say. My dad looks out the window to see the chief still standing next to the car, glaring at us with his arms folded menacingly over his chest.

Dad's blank look slowly turns into a big grin as he squeezes and shakes my shoulder in his strong right hand.

"Now that's the way to stand up for your friends, Josh. You might want to work on your technique a little, but you're getting the idea."

"Technique?"

"Yeah, technique. You can't just go yelling right into somebody's face like that. You have to be more subtle, okay?"

I shrug. "Sure. Subtle. Okay."

"Right. Just be subtle."

With that, my dad shifts the gear back into drive, jams the accelerator down to the floor, and lets out a howl as our car kicks up an enormous blizzard of slush right into the face of the now-hollering Chief Wellstone.

We haven't gotten more than a block when my dad turns his gaze on me and says, "Josh, always remember—"

"I know, Dad. Always remember to stand by your friends."

"Actually, I was going to say always remember to keep your eye on the ball. Forget the target and just keep your eye on the ball!"

We laugh the rest of the way to the golf course.

14

Forty-Three Hours before Sarah's Death

As we approach the limo, a valet is loading Robert's golf clubs into the trunk.

"Oh gimme a break, Robert. I didn't even bring golf shoes, let alone my clubs. And you've got your own gear. That's worth two strokes a side right there."

"Bullshit, son. We're playing straight up. No handicaps today, and the pro shop will set you up with anything you want."

Under my breath, I whisper, "hustler." Robert shoots me a classic sideways sneer. Super Bowl Sunday morning, and the game is already on!

Two hours earlier, when my brief sleep was interrupted by the in-room breakfast being served, I had a hunch this was going to be one of the greatest, maybe *the* greatest, day of my life. Hey, what better wake-up call than a tray of hot bacon, eggs, and croissants? I'll take that any day over another rude awakening from Scappelli. The hotel finally routed his last call straight to my message box. Hopefully, that will be the last I hear from him.

After breakfast, I threw open the curtains and was greeted by a magnificent blue sea glimmering in the morning sun. A beautiful yacht gently bobbed up and down only a few hundred yards off shore. I thought about the money I had made playing craps with Robert the last two days. It was all like a dream.

Our suite came complete with a telescope next to the picture window, and I pointed it at the yacht. It took a minute to get everything in focus, but when I did, I was rewarded with an amazing image of two spectacular young women lying bare-ass naked on the deck. Yeah, this was going to be my best day ever. Golf with Robert, followed by my Redskins in the Super Bowl, and one last return trip to the casino for dessert. Not too shabby! Briefly, I think about returning Phil's call, but it's just too early on a Sunday morning to be waking up a pissed-off guy who went to bed drunk. And I'm not going to let it ruin my day.

I looked over to the bed and saw Sarah still sleeping. She looked beautiful. Something about her seemed different, though, and it took a minute before I realized that it was how peaceful she looked just lying there. Over the past few months, I had grown used to seeing her in pain all the time. For a moment I thought my heart was going to break. I gently sat down on the edge of the bed and began to stroke her hair, short, brown and curly . . . just like it was the day we met.

Sarah's eyes began to flutter and then opened. She slowly turned her head in my direction and gave me a contented smile. Instinctively, I bent toward her, brushed back her bangs, and kissed her forehead.

"I love you so much, Sarah."

Still only half-awake at best, she smiled once more and told me she loved me too. Then, closing her eyes, she rolled away from me and onto her side. Just like that she was asleep again.

Seeing her, so beautiful and peaceful in her sleep, sent fear washing over me like a giant wave. My mind drifted to the worst. What if I lose her too?

This time I whispered so I wouldn't wake her again. "I do love you, Sarah. I love you, I love you, I love you."

The drive to the course takes no more than five minutes, and when the car pulls up to the clubhouse, we are greeted by another spectacular vista of the Caribbean Sea, only this time framing magnificent rolling fairways and greens. If you love golf, and I *love* golf, this view is enough to take your breath away.

That's why I even surprise myself when Robert asks if this isn't the most beautiful golf course I've ever seen.

"Actually, my favorite would have to be Northwest Park back in Indiana."

Robert seems to look right into me for a moment or two. "Was it as green as this?"

"To tell you the truth, I don't even remember. My favorite rounds were when the whole course was covered in snow. Christmas golf in Hammond, Indiana. But I guess this is a close second."

For the briefest moment, I think I see Robert's dark brown eyes getting just a little moist, but then the smile takes over. "Let's head in and get you set up with some proper equipment. I don't want to hear any bitching out of you."

Robert heads to the locker room to change shoes, and we agree to meet on the range. The head pro lets me know that Mr. Saber is treating and that I should help myself to some new Footjoy shoes and whatever clubs I want. He suggests that I try out a set of Wilson Staff irons, which are number one on the professional tour this year, along with a full set of the Staff persimmon woods. They are the most beautiful golf clubs I've ever seen. The pro says that if I like them, they'll be packed up in a travel bag and sent home with me. Okay, they aren't the rusty old MacGregors that were in the garage back in Potomac, but they'll do!

By the time I am fitted for my shoes, clubs, and the rest of the gear, it is nearly ten o'clock and we are due on the tee. When I tell the pro that it is too bad I can't at least warm up a little on the driving range, he just smiles and tells me to head over and take my time. Mr. Saber has blocked out all tee times for a half-hour on either side of us, so not to worry. Why am I surprised?

━━━━━━━

Golf swings are very individual, some would say almost like an autograph or a fingerprint. As I approach the range, I see Robert hitting some high, soft eight-iron fades. When I see that swing, I feel right at home.

"Nice sticks, Josh. You think you can do any damage with those?"

I just smile and start to work my way through the bag, the way my dad taught me years before. First, I hit around six or seven half shots with my eight iron to try and get a feel for tempo. Then, I swing a few full five irons, followed by some three woods, and then, feeling pretty loose, I pull out my new persimmon wood driver and let it rip.

"Yeah, I'd say I'm ready. What are the stakes? Want to go for a friendly little hundred dollar Nassau?" At home I never go higher than five dollars, but what the hell. I'd just won over $150,000, so this was nothing.

"No, Josh. I don't want to take your money. Here's the deal: you win, and I'll wear a Redskins hat tonight when we're watching the game. But in the off, off chance that I win, kick your ass actually, you will proudly wear the blue and orange of the Bears."

"You call that a bet?"

"I call it sporting your true colors, that's all. We Bears fans need all the help we can get!"

We shake on it and approach the first tee. Our crew is made up of Robert, me, and three caddies—one for each of us and a fore-caddy just for good measure, to spot our balls.

Robert throws a tee in the air to see which of us will hit first. The tee spins and, when it falls, points right at him—but then seems to almost do a back flip and settle in my direction. Strange.

As I walk up to the tee markers, I force myself to slow everything down—my pace, my breathing, my every motion. Dad taught me that too, but somehow I'd forgotten it along the way. I tee up my ball and take a few steps back so I can look directly over it and out to the rolling fairway. I picture my shot and picture myself making the swing. I try *not* to think about Robert watching my every move, but I know he is watching, and more importantly, I know he approves.

I have the image of my shot firmly locked in my mind, and without hesitation, I take my stance and begin to draw the club back, low and slow. I keep going until my left shoulder is well behind the ball and my right side is all loaded up. Now, just a momentary pause at the top, and then fire my right knee at the target and let it rip. Just the way he taught me. And there it goes: long, straight, high, with just a hint of a draw as it moves slightly left against the brilliant blue sky. Has to be at least 250 yards. As nice a drive as I've ever hit.

I spin on my heels to face Robert, with the Wilson driver held aloft. "What the hell kind of piece of crap is this you've got me playing with?"

"Don't get too carried away with yourself, hotshot. Lot of golf left to play."

Robert takes the tee and matches my draw with a gorgeous high fade. He hits about ten yards behind me, but by the time the ball has settled down, it's a good fifteen yards ahead.

"Not bad for an old guy."

I smile and start to march down the fairway.

"Whoa! Where do you think you're going? We've got a beautiful day, these fine men to help us around the course, and a friendly bet. Now take this, and the picture is complete."

"Cuban?"

"You bet. Cohiba. The best."

Robert snips off the tips of the cigars, pulls out a gold-trimmed enamel Dunhill lighter, and we fire up.

Okay, I might look just a little stupid in my burgundy slacks, gold Redskins shirt, and seven-inch cigar, but I feel like Sean Connery. James Bond, actually. Robert throws his arm around my shoulders and says, "Now we're ready. Let's go play some golf." And we march off the first tee.

Joy. Pure joy.

———————

Seven holes in, and I'm only two over par. Okay. It's a fairly easy course, but we are playing from the back tees, so I'm pretty pleased. I am also up two holes on Robert, but that doesn't seem to bother him at all.

"Okay, Robert, I'd invite you to press the bet, but since we're betting on team hats, I don't know what the point would be."

"You're on!"

"I'm on for what?"

"I'm pressing the bet. You lose, and you not only wear a Bears hat, but you'll wear their colors too. Same for me if I lose."

"Fine, whatever you say. My swing is grooved, so I'm not too worried."

"Good thing, Josh. Number eight is only 160 yards, but the ocean runs along the entire left side of the hole. You drift a little or come up short and you're wet."

As we approach the eighth tee, I see what he means. The hole is carved right around the shoreline, with nothing separating the tee box and the green but water—water that for the first time doesn't look so beautiful to me.

I take out my five iron and go through my normal preshot routine. I picture the perfect shot in my head, with a flight along the left side of the fairway floating high and soft so that the constant sea breeze will be just enough to bring my ball safely onto the green.

As soon as I hit it, I know it is perfect. The ball flies straight out toward the left side of the green and awaits the off-shore breeze. A moment of waiting seems like forever, but when the wind finally does come, it blows from my right side.

"What?" I yell to no one in particular. "This can't be happening!"

Instead of bringing my beautiful shot safely onto the green, the shifting wind pushes it slowly, but surely, out into the sea.

"Bad break, Josh. You know, sometimes you can do everything right and you still get hit with a little bit of bad luck."

I reach into my pocket for another ball and turn back to Robert with the cocky grin of a competitor.

"I believe in making my own luck."

I re-tee my ball and take my stance. And I am fine until Robert starts talking to me again.

"I'm just saying that even the best of people catch a bad break. Don't let it affect your confidence, Josh. Don't let it get inside your head."

Jeez, is he ever going to stop talking and let me hit? One more waggle of my club.

"Don't even think about the wind, son."

I turn my head again toward Robert and try to maintain my confidence, but I've been standing over the ball a bit too long. That's probably why I jerk the club back and hit as ugly a shot as I've ever seen. Low. Left. And straight to the bottom of the sea.

"One more try, Josh?"

"No thanks. It's your hole, but I'm still up one. Let's move on to number nine."

Over the next few holes, I hit one awful shot after another. When we approach the fourteenth tee, I take my driver and slump down on a bench, waiting for Robert to once again lead the way with his honors. Instead, Robert tells his caddie to give him a minute, and he joins me on the bench.

I try to smile, but that's about as hard to do as hitting a single good shot.

"I've lost my game, Robert."

"You didn't lose your game, son. You just lost your confidence."

Nobody questions my confidence.

"I'm one of the most confident people you'll ever meet." I might have sounded just a tad defensive when I blurted, "You don't get to be one of the top officers of Grand National at thirty-five without having a boatload of confidence."

Robert reacted with a quick bit of a laugh and leaned in even closer to me.

"Oh really, Mr. Grand National. Never a doubt? Never a question about whether you're doing the right thing or not?"

Out of nowhere, an image comes into my head of Phil flying into a rage, but that's crowded out by the pleading voice of Anthony Scappelli. But only for a moment.

"Never any fear, Josh?"

Fear? Now Scappelli's voice gives way to an image of Sarah lying in our bed. So peaceful. So still.

I try to pull it together long enough to fake a grin up at Robert.

"Not really. No. I'm kind of a natural, and that comes from believing in myself. I know I can always count on *me*."

Robert shrugs and looks me in the eye.

"Son, it's pretty tough to be self-confident in your head when your heart isn't sure what to do. Don't let that ten-year-old boy boss you around."

I swallow hard. We sit there in silence for a few minutes. I want to speak, but I just don't know how to explain myself. It's as if he knows me better than I know myself. Finally, Robert sits upright and slaps the knee he'd been holding.

"All right. Enough pouting. I've been watching your pathetic little meltdown ever since your bad break on number eight, and I can't take it anymore. Come over here."

I follow Robert up to the tee box, prepared to do anything he tells me to do, even if it doesn't make any sense to me. That's what a desperate golfer in search of a good swing will do.

Without speaking a word, Robert grips a club with his left hand and then slowly stretches out his left thumb, all the while staring right at me to make sure I am taking this in. He repeats the stretching motion a few more times for emphasis.

"You're kidding! You want me to stretch out my left thumb? That's going to cure my lousy game?"

"Just do it. I guarantee it will work."

I laugh. "I guess I don't have anything to lose."

I stand over the ball and take my regular grip. I swivel my head and take one more look at the flag of the par three gently waving in the wind 178 yards away. Then I stretch out my left thumb, *the greatest golf secret ever told* according to my buddy here. I can feel that my turn and swing are smooth—yeah, that's how it's supposed to feel. I keep thinking about that left thumb and how it would make my whole body extend right through the ball. And then there's that sound, that beautiful, almost imperceptible sound a club makes when it hits a ball pure. I hold my finishing pose and watch the sweetest little shot I've hit all day. It is high and soft, hitting the green about six feet in front of the hole and rolling within a foot of the cup.

As the ball gets closer and closer to the hole, the shot goes from being the prettiest shot I've hit all day to the best I've ever hit in my life. Quite a promotion. I turn to Robert with a look of total wonder. He winks and says, "Close your mouth before the flies get in. Just close your mouth and smile."

Over the remaining holes, Robert reinforces my confidence with each swing I make, always reminding me at the last moment to stretch out my thumb. And each great swing brings me more and more back to my old self. All from a stretched left thumb!

As we approach the eighteenth hole and our match is dead even, I confidently take my honors up to the tee box. As I bend over to tee up my ball, Robert offers one last comment.

"So this is as good a time as any to tell you, Josh."

"Tell me what?"

"Well, no big deal. But that left thumb business is all bullshit."

I turned and stare back at him in disbelief. "So that's what this is all about? You're just messing with my head?"

"I'm not messing with you. I'm telling you that the left thumb stretch was nothing but a gimmick.

"Left thumb, right thumb, little toe. It doesn't matter, Josh. The only thing that matters is that you believe in yourself.

And the next time your golf swing, or anything else for that matter, seems to be deserting you, the next time you become just a little afraid, remember this day and remember that *you* made it happen. Just *you*."

I guess I've never been so pleased to be duped. Left thumb. Amazing. I don't even think about my next words. They just seem to come out of my mouth from somewhere else.

"Robert, where have you been my whole life?"

The silence is more than a little awkward, and I can't bring myself to look him in the eye. It was an accident, but still, have I crossed some kind of line? Has he?

I break the silence. "So now what? Should I cut you some slack and take it easy on you for the last hole?"

"Only if you want to lose, buddy."

My birdie on eighteen shows him that I have no intention of losing. And his matching birdie shows me that he is right there with me. When I hole out my final putt, Robert is there to shake my hand. Our match ends dead even. A perfect ending to a memorable round of golf.

———

The short ride back to the hotel starts in silence, and my mind begins to wander. So far it has been an incredible day, and yet, for some reason, I'm becoming apprehensive. *Scared* is more like it, and I can feel my own sweat against my open collar.

I am thinking about Sarah and the pain she has been experiencing. She's not a complainer, not Sarah.

Oh my God, I'm going to lose her. I'm going to lose the

best part of me. And poor Richie and Sophie. So small. So trusting. So in need of their mother.

Sitting in the back of the limo with Robert leaving me to my own thoughts, I'm overcome with sadness, with emptiness. My stomach aches, a sharp, raw pain.

What have I done? *Nothing.* That's the problem. I've stood by and watched but done nothing, nothing to ease *her* pain. And now what if I lose her? I'm becoming numb with fear, and I try to shake it off.

On the golf course, Robert told me it's okay to be afraid, but that you have to keep on living and trying to do the best you can. I realized that all this time my own cockiness, even my great confidence, was just a mirage. Just a shield to protect the sad little ten-year-old boy that I'd never stopped being.

And what of Scappelli?

No, wait a second. This isn't about Scappelli. It's Sarah that I need to help. Not Scappelli. Not some daughter of a policyholder that I'll never know.

"Are you okay, Josh?"

When I look up, I take Robert by surprise.

"Why, son, you're crying."

I muster a weak smile.

My mind is racing now, the images flashing before my eyes: standing in the cold rain watching the rabbit's foot wash away; Sarah curled in a ball of pain; Richie and Sophie crying. Phil screaming. And Scappelli's pleading voice.

"Robert, before, back on the golf course, I asked you where you've been my whole life. I just need to know. I need to know what's going on here."

Robert puts his hand on my shoulder, smiling sadly. "I'm here now, Josh, aren't I? I'm here now."

I don't say it, but he doesn't need to be a mind reader to know what I'm thinking. *Don't ever leave me. Please, please, don't leave me again.*

15

One Day before My Father Dies

P lease don't send me away, Dad. *Please!* I don't want to go on that stupid trip. Come on, we've got a great hill a block from the house. That's good enough for me."

I'm sitting here in the front seat begging him, but I can tell it isn't working.

"And why is this trip stupid, Josh?"

My dad just keeps smiling and doesn't even look at me. He glances again at the rearview mirror, his knuckles white from gripping the steering wheel so tightly. Once again the roads have iced up overnight, but as we approach the school parking lot, we can see where the trucks have been out sanding. Dad lets out a deep breath and lightens up on the wheel.

"It's stupid because you are paying money for me and Sammy to go on a trip to get the crap kicked out of us. I just don't understand why you are making me go."

"We've been over this a dozen times. First off, you don't run away from bullies. Mickey Wellstone doesn't decide what you do. *You* decide what you do."

"But I'm dead meat with those guys."

"And second, you don't run out on your friends. Just

stick by Sammy. Put your heads together. You guys will figure it out."

"Honest, Dad. I'm really scared."

"Well, then, I guess it's time."

"Time? Time for what?"

Dad reaches behind him and pulls out his lucky rabbit's foot. He holds it up for me to take.

"You're giving me your rabbit's foot? That's your favorite thing in the world. You said that's what got you through the war."

"Well, you're half right. It *is* what got me through the war. But it's not the most important thing to me. You are, and I want you to have it."

I just stare at it, not knowing what to say.

"Hey, Josh, look at it this way: if it protected me from a couple thousand Japs shooting at me, it can certainly get you through a couple days with Mickey. Just have a great time with Sammy, come back safe and sound on Friday, and then on Sunday you and I will have the best day of our lives watching the Bears beat the Giants for the NFL Championship!"

The rabbit's foot hangs on its chain from my fingers. I stare at it like I've never seen it before, rubbing my thumb over the clasp, which is dented and burned where it deflected the bullet from Al's rifle. There isn't anything I can say. I put it in my pocket, but I keep my hand firmly wrapped around it just to make sure it's really there.

With that, Dad turns into the school parking lot. Two buses are parked by the front door, where fifth-grade parents and students are standing around saying their good-byes and unloading the kids' travel bags.

Standing by the first bus is Mickey Wellstone, staring right at me. Robby Burns, one of his goons and the biggest kid in school, is next to him. And lest I have any doubt what is going on, Mickey points right at me while Robby pounds his fist into his other hand. The two of them seem to be having a pretty good laugh. Without even realizing it, I start rubbing the rabbit's foot again, my precious gift from Dad.

As we get out of the car, I look at my dad to see if he is seeing any of this. At first, I think he's staring right at Mickey too, but then I see what he's really looking at. Standing right behind Mickey is his father, Ronnie, and his uncle, Chief Wellstone. Even I can tell that they have it in for my dad just as Mickey does for me.

The battle of the dirty looks might have gone on all morning except for the noise and smell of Mrs. Johnson's car as she pulls into the lot. I've seen cars burning oil before, but her car is leaving a black trail of smoke as long as a football field.

They pull to a stop right next to us. The rear door flies open and Sammy comes bounding out and running straight for me with his arms wide open. He gives me an enormous bear hug that lifts me right off the ground. I guess all is forgiven.

"All right, Sammy, that's enough! Put me down."

A lot of the other kids, and parents too, are looking over at us and at the smelly smoke that finally stops pouring out when Mrs. Johnson turns off the engine.

When Sammy finally lets me go, he turns to my dad and gives him a hug around his waist, looking up with a grin from ear to ear.

"Mr. Brown, my mom says that I should thank you for paying for this trip. She said maybe I could work it off in your store some time?"

"Don't worry about it, Sammy. I'm just glad to see you are a lot happier than the last time I saw you."

"To tell you the truth, I really didn't want to go on this trip, especially with Mickey Wellstone and those guys, but when you said Josh wanted me to come and that he wouldn't go without me, well, I knew I had to come."

What?! Did he say *I* wanted him to come? My grunt of an objection is cut short by the grip my dad suddenly puts on my shoulder. Jeez, that hurts.

"Bob, can I speak to you for a moment please?"

This comes from Sammy's mom through the open window of her car. I look over and see Sammy's big sister, Beth, is slumped down in the back seat. From what I can see, she looks like a mess. Don't tell me that Mickey and his friends beat up Beth too?

My dad puts his face by the open window, but I can't hear what anyone is saying. When he opens the back door, I get a really good look at Beth. Her right eye is all black and puffy. When my dad climbs into the car and sits beside her, she throws her arms around his neck and begins to sob. Now I can hear her, and so can everyone else standing nearby.

She practically screams, "I'm so sorry, Mr. Brown. I'm so sorry. They made me do it. They made me." And then more tears.

I ask Sammy what happened.

"All I know is that about two o'clock in the morning she started banging on our door. I guess her boyfriend told her she had gotten him in trouble with the cops, so he punched her out and told her to get lost."

"What a jerk!"

"I heard Beth tell mom that they've been stealing to get money for liquor for her boyfriend, and she was pretty messed up. Beth told her that one night they were sleeping in his car over in the forest preserve and a cop car pulled up. The cop shined the flashlight right in her boyfriend's eyes so they couldn't see who he was. Then he told her boyfriend to get lost, and when he had Beth alone, he told her they knew all about the stealing and that she'd be going to jail for a very long time, unless she did exactly what they said.

"Beth told my mom that she was so scared, she would do anything he wanted. The cop slapped her hard across the face, and then he ripped off her clothing."

I started to get sick to my stomach. It was Beth who was raped, and my Dad's friend Al was guilty after all.

I finished Sammy's story for him. "So she told the cops who raped her, and they arrested Al. My dad's best friend."

"No, Josh. That's not what happened. The cop told her to stop crying or he'd smack her again. Then he threw her ripped-up clothing at her and told her to get dressed. He said that he would make her a deal. They had a bad cop on the force who was going around hurting women and children, but they couldn't prove it. If she would come down to the station and file a rape complaint and ID the bad cop, that was all she would have to do. So she did what he said, but after that they told her she'd have to leave town and never come back. Or they'd keep her in the lockup until she turned eighteen, and then they'd send her off to prison."

"So she wasn't raped. Al is innocent, like my dad said. This is great, Sammy!"

I'm feeling excited, but Sammy has turned white and is starting to shake a little. I follow his gaze. Chief Wellstone is walking right toward us.

"Dad, watch out!"

My father turns and sees the chief coming too. He must have told Beth to duck down because she disappears from view. Dad is moving pretty quickly now, slamming the backseat door shut just as the chief walks up. He puts his body between the chief and the car, then actually puts his hand up to block the chief's path.

"Get out of my way, Brown."

"There's no reason for you to be hassling Mrs. Johnson, Chief. She's got enough to worry about without you piling on."

"People are ready to vomit from the black cloud she's trailing behind her. I'm going to write her up."

"Listen, I've got to tell you something."

Dad motions Mrs. Johnson from behind his back to fire up her car and get going, but she seems frozen, watching them. He even puts his hand on Chief Wellstone's chest to keep him from moving closer to the car. The chief strains his neck to look over Dad's shoulder.

"Come on, Chief. There's something you need to know."

"Yeah, what is it, Brown?"

"I'm not sure, but Mrs. Johnson was saying something about her missing daughter, Beth."

I'm surprised the chief's head doesn't snap off the way he whips it around. Then all the color goes out of his face, and he starts to fidget with his collar.

"She said you guys were looking for Beth on suspicion of petty theft."

With that, the chief pushes once more to get past my dad.

"Look," my dad says. "She's not going to tell you anything because this is her kid we're talking about and you scare the shit out of her. Just let her go and I'll call you by lunchtime with Beth's location, and I'll make sure she stops burning oil too."

The chief looks my dad in the eyes and then looks at his watch.

"You've got two hours. Two hours to tell me where that little tramp is or I'll write up old lady Johnson as a nuisance and I'll throw your sorry ass in the can for obstruction of justice. Do we understand each other?"

"Don't worry. I know exactly what I'm doing."

After the chief leaves, my dad whispers to Mrs. Johnson something about meeting her at the store in fifteen minutes. She starts up her car, and then with a bang and another cloud of black smoke, Mrs. Johnson yells to Sammy to have a good time and heads out of the lot.

Dad tells Sammy and me to grab our bags, and he walks us over to the bus.

"Dad, can the chief really throw you in jail?"

He gives me that silly grin of his. "I'll be fine. This whole mess will be over by noon, and you can put another one in the books for the good guys."

Dad tosses our bags into the open storage bin under the bus. Ronnie Wellstone is doing the same with Mickey's bag, and Dad gives Ronnie an enormous smile.

"Hi, Ronnie. What a treat seeing you here. I just had the

nicest conversation with your brother, and now I get to see you too."

I can tell that Ronnie is ready to lose it, but he must have seen Dad talking to the chief, and he is probably dying to find out what happened.

My dad looks down at Mickey.

"Hi there, Mickey, look at you. You're not quite as tall as I thought you'd be by now. But don't worry, you'll catch up to the other kids one of these days."

My dad playfully messes up Mickey's hair as Mickey squirms away. Then Dad looks him right in the eye. "And you boys play nice. We'd hate to see your own uncle have to arrest you, after all! Isn't that right, Ronnie?"

Mickey can't tell if my dad is joking or not, but I've never seen him any madder as he turns away and boards the bus without even saying good-bye to his dad.

Dad puts one arm on Sammy's shoulders and one on mine. He gives us each a quick hug and pushes us toward the steps of the bus.

"Have a great time, Josh. It's going to be like one big party!" Dad waves.

I feel for the rabbit's foot one more time and wave back as the bus pulls away. Maybe this won't be so bad after all. A couple days of sledding and then back home to watch the Bears' championship game with Dad.

Let the party begin.

16

Thirty-Five Hours before Sarah's Death

L et the party begin.

Robert opens the door to his suite before I even have a chance to knock. Strange.

"Oh my God." Sarah and I shout out at the same time .

Robert's suite, which is even more spectacular than our own, has been transformed into a temple—a Super Bowl temple fit for worshipping at the altar of the Washington Redskins.

The entire room is decorated with floor-to-ceiling burgundy and gold bunting. The buffets, which are loaded with every possible junk food, have matching tablecloths, not to mention plates, cups, hats, and favors. Everything in the entire suite is done over in burgundy and gold. Everything, that is, except for Robert, who stubbornly wears the blue and orange of the Bears.

Robert gives Sarah a quick hug.

"Do you approve, young lady?"

"Robert, it's fantastic, but how many people have you invited? There's food and favors everywhere. I thought it was just going to be us?"

"It is just us, sweetie. Just us. Just like family."

That *family* line is a bit much for Sarah, who shoots me

a look of mock panic as Robert turns toward the bar to get us each a drink. There is a real spring to his step. He is clearly excited. He looks like he's going to burst with joy as he hands us each a glass of champagne.

Then he motions for us all to lift our glasses. "Champagne, hot dogs, burgers, and chili! A Super Bowl feast *made in heaven*. And since I have no horse in this race, let me just say, ALL HAIL TO THE REDSKINS!"

"Hail to the Redskins!"

We clink glasses, and I thank him. "I'll even say that I hope next year it's for you." One more clink of the glasses as I add, "Bear down, Chicago Bears!"

With that, Robert practically throws himself down on the sofa in front of the television and pats the seats on either side of him for us to join him.

This is it. The day I've been looking forward to since I was a little boy, the day that was stolen from me so many years ago.

Now, here I am. Me, Sarah, and my . . . and Robert. Super Bowl XVII is live from the Rose Bowl on NBC, with Dick Enberg hosting the coverage. As the broadcast begins, I'm not sure who is happier, Robert or me. Even Sarah, who looks more beautiful than ever, seems to be enjoying herself, and her pain seems to be gone, at least for the moment.

As if on cue, Robert jumps up and stands over us.

"Okay, everybody up! Get up, get up! It's the national anthem."

I follow Robert's lead and cover my heart with my hat. Sarah motions with a nod of her head for me to look over at our host. Robert is singing at the top of his lungs, and it is pretty clear from the tears in his eyes that these aren't mere words to him.

At the end of the anthem, we've barely been seated a second when Robert jumps up again, pointing to the TV and screaming. "That's Crazy Legs! Elroy *Crazy Legs* Hirsch is doing the coin toss."

"Crazy Legs?" Sarah asks.

"Crazy Legs Hirsch was a famous old Bear," I explain. "Robert here was probably friends with his grandfather or somebody."

"Very funny, wise guy. And for your information, Crazy Legs never played for the Bears. He played for the Chicago Rockets from 1946 to 1948, right after we—"

Robert stops himself short.

I finish for him.

"Right after you got home from the war. Isn't that right, Robert?"

If he hears me, he gives no sign. He just settles himself back down onto the sofa and stares straight ahead at the screen. I settle in too, just like the old days. And now I know what true contentment means. Here I am with Robert and Sarah. It's as if I'm in my old basement back in Hammond with my dad, only Sarah is here too, making it all the more special. And then it hits me. I need to be making my own memories with Richie and Sophie.

I guess Robert senses that I am staring at him even if I don't realize it myself.

"Need anything, son?"

"Maybe a Barcalounger. Got one of those lying around this dump?"

Robert just chuckles and turns back to the screen to see the opening kick-off. Here we go!

Now, a lot of skill goes into predicting the outcomes of football games. And since I'm in the business of predicting outcomes, I've always held the Las Vegas odds makers in high regard. That doesn't mean they are perfect, of course. Nobody gets it right all the time, and I know that today in particular will be one of the exceptions.

The odds makers all favor Miami in this game, with the Redskins a three-point underdog. I *know* they have this one wrong. I know that the special teams alone will see to that, but it turns out that those teams aren't even the best part. The best part is running back John Riggins having the best game of his life. Good enough to be named the game's MVP. Good enough to get me through three more chili dogs and a bottle of champagne.

Good enough to see the Redskins cruise to a 27-to-17 victory! What a day.

Despite the great game, and the best TV viewing of the year, I notice toward the end that Sarah is rubbing her forehead and closing her eyes. Still, whenever I ask her if she is okay, she just smiles and tells me that everything is fine. Now that the game is over, though, I can tell that Sarah is ready to head straight for bed.

Robert has noticed too, and even though I'm a little tipsy from knocking off my own bottle of champagne, I can see that he's very concerned.

"Okay, guys, that's it for the night. Josh, get that beautiful wife of yours out of here and back into her own bed, where I'm sure she'll feel a lot better."

I nod my agreement.

"Sarah and I already talked about it, Robert. I'll take

her back to the room, and then I'll be right back knocking on your door so we can make our grand entrance into the casino together. *Look out, boys.* We're about to make another sizeable withdrawal!"

Robert walks over and puts his hand on my shoulder.

"You know what, Josh? I don't think so."

My mouth falls open, and even Sarah raises her eyes to see if he is joking.

"You're kidding, right? We talked about this all day, Robert. First the golf, then the game, and then you and I kill the crap tables one more time. What's the deal?"

"The thing is, I don't think we can do any better than this," Robert says as he gestures at the room with a sweep of his arm.

"I mean, it's been a perfect day, topping off a perfect weekend. Being here with you and Sarah, the dinners, the laughs, the golf, the craps, and now this great game that we got to share."

Robert looks me in the eye.

"Really, Josh. It's been a perfect, *perfect* night, and I don't think we can do any better than this."

Still a little tipsy, I just ask him again, "You're kidding, right?"

"You know what? Sometimes it's not about getting more of a good thing. Most of the time we just really need to appreciate the good things we already have."

"But we're leaving tomorrow." I can hear the panic in my voice. "And there's so much more that I, . . . that I, . . . I mean, that I need to know."

My voice just trails off, and I can feel the lump in my throat. It can't end like this.

"Look, Josh, let's meet for breakfast in the morning, okay? Eight o'clock sharp in the lobby café. We'll sort everything out then."

He is gently but firmly moving me and Sarah toward the now-open door. Sarah leads the way, but as I reach the door, his strong grip on my arm stops me in my tracks.

When I turn to face him, he gives me a crushing hug. Then he stretches out his arms and looks me over from head to toe, with a sad smile. The smile leaves his face as he looks over my shoulder to Sarah.

"I know it hurts, Sarah, but don't worry. It won't hurt much longer."

And then he slowly closes the door.

I put my arm around Sarah's waist to support her, and we make our way down the hall, silently now, each with our own pain. I spend the rest of the night doing all I can to ease Sarah's pain. And I wait. I wait until eight o'clock tomorrow morning. I wait until I meet Robert once more. Eight a.m. I wait.

17

One Day before My Father Dies

Everybody in Hammond knows what happened. As the story goes, my dad put Sammy and me on the bus and headed right over to the store, where Mrs. Johnson and Beth were sitting with my mom in the small, windowless office, where they couldn't be seen.

At just about eight o'clock straight up, my dad came into the office and went directly to Beth's side. They said that as soon as my dad touched her shoulder, she buried her head in his chest and began to cry. I guess my dad took a long time, holding her tight, rubbing her hair, telling her that she was safe now and everything was going to be all right. Through her tears, Beth told my mom and dad what had happened to her.

For months Beth and her boyfriend had been living out of his car. All they cared about was getting money, mostly so her boyfriend could get drunk. Sometimes they'd get money from begging, but mostly from stealing, and then they'd head off to the liquor store. If there was any money left over, they'd buy some food, maybe even rent a room somewhere for a few nights.

Beth said that the worst night of her life happened just like Sammy had told me, starting with the sheriff finding them in the forest preserve and scaring off her boyfriend. But, Sammy didn't know the whole story either. It's true that the sheriff slapped her and ripped off her clothes before he told her to get dressed. And I guess that Beth never did get a really good look at his face behind the glare of the flashlight. But when he briefly left her and returned to his own squad car, Beth could see that he wasn't alone. As she dressed, the sheriff opened his car door, sending a flood of light throughout the sedan, and she could clearly see the man sitting alone in the backseat. Beth told my dad that she'd seen this man around town many times. She told him he was there in the parking lot when Sammy and I left for our sledding trip.

My dad thought that Beth was talking about the chief, but Beth set him straight. "No, Mr. Brown, it wasn't Chief Wellstone who was with that sheriff. It was the man who was with the chief this morning."

"Who, Ronnie? Ronnie Wellstone was with the sheriff's officer that night?" Beth wiped her nose with her sleeve and nodded.

She said that when she was all dressed, she got out and stood by the side of her car until the sheriff led her with a firm grasp on her arm over to the squad car. He told her to just get in the front seat with him and to shut up. She'd be told what she needed to do if she didn't want to spend the next fifteen years in prison. And he told her not to look in the backseat.

She was so scared that she started shivering. Her teeth began to chatter, even though it was warm in the squad car. The man in the backseat reached over her shoulder and started to hand her something. She made a motion to turn around, which was met with a sharp open hand to the back of her head courtesy of the sheriff seated next to her.

The man in the back of the car said, "Beth, honey, you're doing fine. Now do you recognize the man in this picture?"

Beth just slowly nodded and braced herself for another slap to the head, but nothing happened.

"That's good. Now, can you tell me his name?"

Beth told them that all she knew was that he was the Jewish policeman she'd seen around from time to time but that she didn't remember his name.

Then from the backseat: "That's Officer Kaplan, Beth. That's the man who scared off your boyfriend tonight and then hurt you. Isn't that right?"

She was crying now, and she was shaking so hard that she barely noticed another sharp rap to the back of her head. She remembered hearing, "Shit, Ronnie, this little bitch just peed herself! My car's gonna smell like warm piss, dammit!"

The sheriff was so mad that he didn't even notice he'd yelled out Wellstone's name, but it didn't matter much anyway since she knew all along who the man in the backseat was, even if she didn't know his name at the time. She figured that Mr. Wellstone didn't care much about the mess she'd made because he just kept on talking to her in that same flat voice.

"That's right. It's Officer Kaplan. The man that scared your boyfriend off. The man that made you get into the backseat with him. The one that ripped off your clothes. The man that raped you. Now isn't that right, Beth?"

She was too scared to even speak. She cried harder, and the sheriff kept swearing about the mess she'd made, but Ronnie just kept on talking.

"That's okay, honey. We all know you've been through a horrible thing, being raped and all. Ain't that right, Beth?"

Her hesitation cost her one more slap to the back of her head. Even harder now because the sheriff was real mad.

"Now don't you worry. All you have to do is let the sheriff here drive you to the station house, where he'll tell the others that he found you wandering around with your clothes half ripped off and that you told him you were raped by Officer Kaplan. Then they'll bring you some warm food and clean clothes and let you rest until they bring Kaplan in, and all you'll have to do is point to him from the other side of some one-way glass. He won't even be able to see you, honey, and you'll be doing this town a real favor since he's such a bad man. After that we'll get you some spending money, have you sign some papers, and then you'll be free to go. Now isn't that better than going to jail for the next fifteen years, Beth?"

So my dad asked Beth if that's just the way it happened, and she started crying all over again. Crying and saying how sorry she was over and over.

By ten a.m. my dad was able to get the mayor to come over to the store so he could talk to Beth and Mrs. Johnson himself. I guess it didn't take much for the mayor to see that the whole thing about Al was just a big lie. And if there was any doubt, when my dad brought Al into the office, the mayor saw the look on her face when she saw how beat up Al was. Al could see that she was trying to apologize, but that she couldn't even speak through all the tears, so he just went to her side and knelt down to tell her it was going to be all right now.

Beth reached out her hand and gently touched Al's bandaged head.

"I'm so sorry. They told me that I was going to go to jail for fifteen years if I didn't lie about you. I'm sorry."

But that was all she could say. From that point on, her sobs became softer and softer, and Al pulled her to him and rocked her like she was a little baby.

They say that there was a lot of crying going on in that little office that day, but my mom told me later that the part she remembers the most was seeing the mayor blowing his nose and wiping away his own tears after telling Al that the charges would be dropped by noon and that he could expect a full written apology from Chief Wellstone, which would be published on the front page of the *Hammond Times* the next morning.

Mom told me later that the mayor even told Al he would be welcome back on the police force any time he wanted, but Al turned him down right on the spot.

"Mr. Mayor, we all know it doesn't work like that in a place like Hammond. I'll just take that written apology so that my name is cleared, but my days as a policeman are over. Besides, my buddy Bob here needs my help to keep this little business afloat."

I guess at that point my dad jumped in. "Well, it's all settled then. And Beth looks like she could use a good meal. Let's all head over to Giovanni's for some breakfast. The city will pay. Isn't that right, Mr. Mayor?"

"I'd say the city got off easy, Bob. Breakfast time, everybody!"

18

Twenty-One Hours before Sarah's Death

Breakfast time, Sarah!"

We settle into a nice corner booth, with me facing the door so I can wave down Robert the minute he comes in. Sarah is right across from me, with a nice window view of the Britannia's front entrance and the long line of just about every limo in Nassau.

From off to my side comes a chorus of laughter. A mother and father with their young son and daughter are all laughing as one. Their little boy, who is just about Richie's age, has a teaspoon balanced on the tip of his nose. I motion Sarah to watch them as well.

Without taking my eyes off of their table, I say, "Why don't we plan a little getaway with the kids when we get home? Maybe a little sledding and skiing over in West Virginia."

"Josh, it is so great to see you like this. I'm getting to like that stupid smile you've got constantly plastered from ear to ear."

I put down my menu and stare intently into Sarah's beautiful face. She looks so fresh and pure, like a little girl in her cute sundress. But something still isn't quite right. Her smile is strained through the now near-constant pain of her recurring headaches, and lately her vision has become blurred—when trying to read a book or even the menu she holds in her hand. God, how I love her. And now that I'm finally letting her into my heart, it hurts just to see her suffering. Maybe I was better off before in my own little world, where I was nice and safe. Just me and my data from the office.

I go back to the menu, where everything, and I mean everything, looks good to me.

"I'm starving, Sarah. Where is he, anyway? I don't know what I want more right now, seeing Robert, or a plate of bacon and eggs." I can't even look up from the menu long enough to focus on the strained voice that comes back to me.

"Josh." And then a little more urgently, "Josh!"

I tilt my menu down and see Sarah staring out the window. I follow her gaze just as a man's leg is swinging into the backseat of a limo. The uniformed doorman gives a smart salute and closes the door. It was only a leg, but I know by the horrified look on Sarah's face who it was as the car pulls away from the hotel and onto the main road.

"That's Robert in that car, isn't it, Sarah?"

She just nods, never taking her eyes from the window, even as the limo makes its turn and is out of sight.

"He looked right at me, Josh. He was surrounded by people who were coming and going, but he looked right through them like he could clear a path with his eyes, and he looked right at me. He just smiled, a sad, sad smile, and got into the car."

I sit bolt upright. "And now he's gone." Angrier now, I repeat, "And now he's gone!"

A Gift from My Father

I feel a presence even before I see a figure looming over me. Only when he clears his throat the second or third time do I begrudgingly look up to see my old buddy Bainsworth standing at my side.

"Good morning, Mr. Brown." And then a nod to Sarah. "Mrs. Brown, I trust all is well?"

But it isn't a genuine question, just a formality before the business at hand. He bends forward and puts an envelope on the plate in front of me, gives a smart little bow from the neck, and briskly turns and walks away.

I pick up the envelope and just stare at it for the longest time. It is simply marked *Josh*.

———————

Dear Josh,

In time I hope you'll forgive me for not leaving you this morning with a proper good-bye, but you see, my time was up, and I had no choice.

I know you are confused. I know you want closure. I know you're asking if somehow a miracle happened here the past few days and whether you just somehow spent Super Bowl weekend with the father that you lost. You're asking yourself if your father came back from the dead. And I'll give you the best answer I can.

But first, let me just say that if I was your father, I would be proud of you. But to tell you the truth, you have a long way to go to be the man that I know you can be. More than twenty-five years ago, without warning, your whole world changed, and your father, your hero, left you. I know he told you that he'd always be there for you, but then suddenly one day he wasn't. I just want to say that I know he didn't lie to you. Your father honestly believed that he would always be there for you, or at least for as long as you needed him. But then again, I guess you could say that he didn't know everything.

Here's the thing: your father loved you with all his heart. So much so that if a miracle could happen, if he really could come back to you, well, maybe somehow he'd find a way. Especially if you were in need. And Josh you are in need.

Now don't get me wrong here. Many fathers would be very proud of you just the way you are. You're a very smart guy and that's led you to be successful too, at least by your own measure. But having spent the last few days with you, I have to tell you that you really aren't that successful. At least not where I come from.

Josh, it brings me no pleasure to say this, but if ever there was a man who couldn't see the forest for the trees, it's you.

I slam my fist on the table hard enough to send my silverware flying. Sarah jumps, and heads at nearby tables snap to stare. I look up at Sarah and snarl in my most sarcastic voice, "Robert says I can't see the forest from the trees."

Sarah has no color in her face. She bends over to pick up a fallen fork from the floor and smiles nervously at the gawkers from the next table. I pick up reading where I'd left off.

You spend nearly every waking hour thinking about your job, trying to figure out everything there is to know about how different groups of people act, and then what will happen to them. And why? Because you want to make sure that your company doesn't have to help the people in these groups. People that you don't even see. People that to you are just numbers on a big printout someplace.

Face it: the only people that you really know about are a bunch of football players. Sadly, you know more about them then you do about your own wife and kids.

Am I saying that you are some kind of horrible person? No, I'm not. What I'm saying is that more than twenty-five years ago, you lost someone who meant the whole world to you, and sadly, you swore never to be hurt again. You swore that no one would ever get close enough to you to allow that to happen.

But fortunately, life doesn't work that way. You met Sarah, and you did fall in love with her, even if you think you just needed each other. I can see that you are truly in love with her, just from the past few days. And I know you love Richie and Sophie, too, even if you haven't taken a good look lately.

So just look at them, Josh! Really look at Richie. Look at how badly he'd like you to come to one of his soccer games. Look at Sophie. She barely knows who you are. But if you don't do anything else, take a really good look at Sarah. She's right in front of you, and you don't even see her.

If you think I am your father, then you probably think that I owe you one, and you'd be right. Either way, I have a gift for you, a very precious gift. The gift of life.

Sarah is sick, and you may lose her. Don't ask yourself how I know this. Just trust me that it's true. When you get back to D.C., on the very next plane, you need to get in touch with a Dr. Thomas Bowman at the National Institutes of Health. I've written his private office number below. He's a good man, and he is developing a new surgical procedure that may be Sarah's only hope. You are one of the few people in the world who has ever heard of this procedure. It's the Level Three Intervention. And since you know about it, you know that it's still experimental, dangerous even. But Josh, you have no choice.

I'm giving you a chance here. A chance that can save Sarah. A chance to be a real husband and a real father. A chance to open your eyes to what you need to do and the kind of man you need to be. The kind of man your father wants you to be. It's okay to be afraid. It's just not a reason to stop living and to pretend you are someone other than who I know you really are.

Oh, and one more thing. The question isn't whether your father came back from the dead. Your father never left you. He's been with you all along.

Fondly,
Robert

———

I sit back in the booth and let out a heavy sigh.

My father never left me? I'm not the kind of man I should be? And best of all, *Sarah needs the bullshit Level Three?* This guy is just messing with me. What a jerk!

Looking at my outstretched arm with the letter still in my hand, I think, this can't be happening to me again. That's not even *my* arm, and that can't be *my* hand holding that piece of paper. *And it certainly isn't my letter!*

That arm and hand, whoever they belong to, crumple the letter into a tight ball and throw it down.

That's not my arm. That's not my hand. And that's not my letter.

The only thing that is mine is the anger. Sonofabitch. Sonofabitch! What an idiot I am. He's done it to me again!

I swat the crumpled letter off the table and onto the floor a good ten feet away. More angry looks from the people seated around us, but I couldn't care less.

The hell with him. The hell with Sarah and her stupid sister too. I shoot an angry look over at Sarah, but she isn't even looking at me. She's rubbing her forehead with both hands and whispering, "Josh, I need to go home now. I need to go home."

―――――――――

As we finish packing for the trip home, I take a quick break to call Phil. He needs to know that when it comes to derailing Level Three, I haven't taken my eye off the ball.

"Morning, boss. I just wanted to touch base with you before jumping on the flight home. I'll be back in the office by midday to tie up any loose ends on Level Three."

Phil still sounds angry. "It's good that you called me. While you were enjoying your little outing, I was locked up with our outside counsel. Don't plan on getting out of the office anytime soon this week. We need to clean house."

"Sorry, but I'm not following you. What does clean house mean?"

I can hear the ice in his voice.

"You're a lawyer. Do I have to spell it out for you? We have paperwork lying around that we need to get rid of. Correspondence, faxes, reports. Documents—many with your name on them, by the way—that would better serve us if they didn't exist."

"Our lawyers actually told you we need to destroy some documents?"

"Josh, I'm not sure I like the tone of your voice. I'm sitting here thinking you're on the team. This is crunch time, my friend, and that's no place for fence sitters."

We must have been served with a subpoena on Friday as part of an investigation. And he's right; my name would be smack in the middle of this mess.

Is he seriously asking me to break the law? Not that I want to be a practicing attorney, but I could get disbarred, or worse, for destroying evidence.

His sharp tone brings me back to the present.

"In or out, it's your call, but don't walk into my office today unless you know. Do we understand each other here?"

"I'm in. I'm in! I just didn't know it had gotten to this point. I'm in, Phil, and I'm sorry if I caused you any doubt."

Silence on the other end just to make me sweat it out.

"All right, then. That's the Josh I know. Now show up fresh. We have a lot of work to do to get this damned thing killed."

And the line goes dead.

19

The Day My Father Dies

The way the story goes, my dad and Al had the time of their lives, after an emotional day that included the mayor signing a declaration issuing an official apology to Officer Al Kaplan for "the wholly unwarranted accusations that had been made against this fine and loyal servant and defender of the good people of Hammond, Indiana."

After the satisfaction of watching a furious and red-faced Chief Wellstone offering, at the mayor's direct order, to reinstate Officer Kaplan to immediate active duty, which was promptly but politely declined, my dad and Al, two lifelong buddies, headed off together to the Tavern Inn on Ridge Road for the best steaks and the stiffest drinks in town.

According to the article in the *Hammond Times*, my dad and Al arrived at the restaurant right around eight p.m. and spent the next four hours eating and drinking and then drinking some more, courtesy of just about every patron in the restaurant. Nearly everyone in the place admired my dad. They wanted to offer their congratulations and, I suppose, an unspoken apology or two for even listening to Wellstone's side of the story. The article said the entire dining room was in good cheer during this impromptu celebration of Al's vindication by a large group of locals who could rightly be called "fair weather fans." It was sort of the way my dad described any Southsider who pulled for the Cubs over the White Sox.

Reading the article, I get the impression that this party could have gone on all night long, and maybe that was because the crowd included so many local big shots. But at 12:01 a.m., Gus, the owner, turned the lights way up and stood by the open front door to a loud chorus of boos; with a big smile and a circling arm, he indicated the general direction of the parking lot.

"Come on, everybody, out. Out! I'm freezing here. OUT!"

Amid the good-natured grumbling and the mass exodus toward the cars, Al told my dad he had to make a pit stop. My dad was more or less pushed along with the crowd into the parking lot. He yelled back to Al that his stalling was probably just an excuse so my dad would get the car preheated. Al hollered back, "There's nothing like the heater in a Chevy!" as he disappeared into the men's room.

The report said my dad was just about at the car, keys in hand, when a very drunk Ronnie Wellstone pushed him from behind and sent him sprawling on the icy ground. When my dad began to get up, he was visibly shocked to see that Ronnie had a gun out. Ronnie's hand was pretty shaky, but the gun was more or less pointed at my father's head.

I guess Ronnie was so drunk that he didn't even seem to notice that most of the large crowd from the restaurant was standing close by. The article even said that the parking lot was well lit. The whole drama played out like some kind of surreal staged production.

"Go home, Ronnie," my dad said as he slowly got to his feet on the slick, icy ground. "Just put that gun down and go on home."

"You couldn't leave things alone, could you, Brown? You couldn't mind your own goddamn business."

They said that Ronnie was glassy eyed, almost like he was in a trance, and that he didn't even respond to the other voices around him also telling him to put down that gun. At least they thought he hadn't heard them until he pointed the gun straight up into the air and pulled the trigger. The shot was enough to silence the crowd and make them quickly duck behind their cars. And just as quickly, Ronnie leveled the gun back at my father, even as his feet tried to steady themselves on the ice.

"This is all your fault. You had to bring that Jew here to Hammond. You should have left him in Chicago with the other Jews."

"Put the gun down, Ronnie."

I don't know if it was the tone of the voice or if Ronnie recognized it, but for the first time he turned his head away from my dad and over to Al, who stood only ten feet away. Al had the little gun from his ankle holster outstretched, pointed right at Ronnie's chest, just as they'd taught him first in the army and later at the police academy. But Ronnie never pointed the gun away from my dad. His head darted back and forth between the two men he blamed for ruining his life and killing his golden goose.

"Oh, this is just great!" My dad yelled. "I've got a drunk pointing a gun at me and the worst shot in the United

States Army is coming to my rescue! Why don't the both of you rocket scientists just put down those guns and let's all go home to our nice warm beds? That's where I'm going."

With that, my dad turned and moved to put his keys in the car door. He never saw that Al was moving even closer to Ronnie. My dad alone among the twenty-plus witnesses didn't see as Ronnie jerked his head back toward Al—jerked so quickly that he lost his footing on the ice. My dad didn't see the shot that was fired when Ronnie's gun went off. He didn't see the second shot either—the shot Al fired that, for once, hit its intended target.

20

Twelve Hours before Sarah's Death

A fter coming into the house from the garage, the first thing I notice is how quiet everything is. Sherry has taken the kids over to her house so Sarah can get some rest.

We made the flight home in silence, too. I was still furious. "Mad at the world" would be a fair way to put it. I was mad at Sarah for her constant complaining. I was mad at Robert, whoever the hell he was, for screwing me up all over again. He'd even made me question my own self-confidence, for God's sake, saying the ten-year-old inside me was calling all the shots. But mostly I was mad at myself. Hadn't I learned my lesson? Hadn't I learned anything from my father's death?

I don't realize how tired I am until after I've practically carried Sarah from the car into our family room, where she collapses on the sofa. I throw myself into the adjoining loveseat, but the second my ass sinks in, the phone in the kitchen lets out an incredibly loud and shrill ring. Dammit, Richie must have been playing with it. I scramble into the kitchen and grab the phone off the wall.

"Hello?"

"Hello, Mr. Brown. Anthony Scappelli here."

"You're kidding, right? I suppose the next thing you're going to tell me is that you're right outside my door."

"No, Mr. Brown. I'm still in Baltimore. Only now I'm calling you from the St. Agnes Hospital. The St. Agnes charity hospital that is."

"Sorry, but I don't know it." I am too tired to even be angry with this man.

"No, you wouldn't, would you? Good news for you, though. This will be the last time that I call you. My little girl, my little Angela, probably won't last another day. I just wanted you to know, that's all."

My heart skips a beat. I'm not sure what to say.

"I hope, Mr. Brown, I hope that not even you have to go through the pain of losing someone that you love so much."

I swallow hard.

"Look, Mr. Scappelli, I'm—"

"Good-bye, Mr. Brown." And the line goes dead.

I sit down at the kitchen table and rest my head in my folded arms. I am exhausted. The trip. Robert. Sarah. Scappelli. I just don't know anymore. I left Washington three days ago so sure of myself. Life was simple and easy for me. Just trust the data. The data never lie. The data will never hurt me. Now, I just don't know.

I must have fallen asleep right there at the table. I wake to a crashing sound from the family room that sounds like a freight train has burst through the house.

I run back into the family room and see an end table turned on its side. The broken glass from its top is scattered in a thousand pieces around a toppled pole lamp and Sophie's Cabbage Patch doll. And there is

Sarah, passed out on the floor and white as fresh snow.

I bend down by her side and try to wake her, but she isn't responding. I put my ear by her face, and it sounds like she is barely breathing.

My first thought is to call for an ambulance, but as I start to get up, I see something else on the floor. Something that I recognize right off. Just beyond Sarah's outstretched hand is the note from Robert that I had crumpled up and thrown away back in the restaurant this morning. But this can't be. The letter on our floor is as crisp and new as when I first read it. How is this possible?

Shaking now, I reach for the open letter and my eye goes right to the bottom of the page, right to where Robert had written Dr. Bowman's private number.

I know what I have to do. No more confusion. No more false confidence protecting a scared little boy. This is my Sarah lying in front of me. This is my life, and if I don't act now, I'll lose her forever.

———————

"Yes, hello, Mr. Brown. This is Tom Bowman. I've been expecting your call. In fact my surgical team is all assembled. We actually thought you'd be here by now."

My mind is racing, and nothing is making sense. I close my eyes and try to think, but all I can remember is Robert's face smiling back at me.

"Mr. Brown? Are you there?"

"I'm here, doctor. I just don't understand. This is all happening so quickly."

"Quickly? Mr. Brown, we've had your wife's paperwork

for the Level Three Intervention surgery in place for weeks now. And your family physician, Dr. Saber, I believe his name is, called today to say that Sarah's condition has become even more critical."

"Dr. Saber, you say? Dr. Robert Saber?"

"Dr. Robert Saber. Sounds like a remarkable man, and a man who must know all the right people too. When I was first handed your wife's file, it came straight from the director of the NIH himself. And when I asked him where he'd gotten it, the director pointed a finger straight up and said it was coming 'right from the top.'"

My mind continues to race. Who is Robert, really? I look down at Sarah, but she barely stirs, even as I cradle her in my arms.

"Dr. Saber knows that Level Three is still unproven too. He sent me over a note this afternoon, saying science is great, but a little luck doesn't hurt either. He included a small rabbit's foot key chain. I haven't seen one of these in years."

The mention of the rabbit's foot brings a smile to my face. I suddenly feel reassured that Sarah will be safe.

"Dr. Bowman?"

"Yes?"

"The NIH is a big place. What building exactly are you in?"

21

The Day My Father Died

After an hour in the arts and crafts tent, all the kids have the morning free, so Sammy and I head over to the nearest slope for our first sledding of the day. And this is shaping up to be a pretty good day, too, starting with breakfast. This morning, for the first time ever, I ate more food than Sammy. I had nine pancakes. He only managed seven.

The snow is pretty deep all across the campground, but with my high boots on, it is fun to walk and kick up little blizzards. Sammy is moving a little slower; he has on the old boots my dad gave him, which are about four sizes too large, with socks balled up in the toes to make them a little tighter. But we each have one hand on the pull rope, and the sled easily follows behind us. In his other hand, Sammy totes a fat tree branch, practically a log, which he is using as a walking stick. We are quite a pair. And we laugh, not for any reason, just walking, kicking up the snow, and laughing.

And then it begins.

The trees are getting bigger and closer together, so when Mickey and his two friends step out to block our path, they are only about twenty feet in front of us.

Mickey stands in the middle. Robby and Mitch are doing their best to strike a pose like tough guys, with their arms folded over their chests. Mickey is pounding his fist into the palm of his hand and smirking.

"Hello again, girls. It's so nice to see you here in *our* woods." Robby and Mitch's laughter cuts right through me.

At that point, I notice that I've thrust my hand deep in my pocket, squeezing my Dad's rabbit's foot as hard as I can. Sammy has raised his sturdy walking stick and holds it now in two hands out in front of him, level with his chest.

He is staring right at me. "You okay, Josh?"

"Yeah, I'm okay, Sammy. I'm with you."

Sammy gives me the biggest smile I've ever seen. "I knew you'd come back for me. I just knew it!"

"What are you girls smiling about? Don't you know what's coming?" Mickey just can't stand that we aren't scared.

Sammy shoots right back at him without even hesitating. "We're not afraid of you guys. You're the ones that ought to be afraid. Just think how embarrassed you're all going to be when the other kids find out that Josh and I kicked your butts. Two against three, too. It doesn't even matter."

With that, Sammy takes the smallest step forward, and I see a flash of fear in Mickey's eyes. I rub the rabbit's foot even faster to keep the spell, or whatever it is, working.

Mickey raises his arm up and points his finger right at Sammy. His voice cracks at first, but the words are clear enough. "You don't even have a father, fat boy." And then he starts chanting, "No father. No father." Faster and louder now, with Robby and Mitch all pointing at Sammy, they yell over and over, "No father, no father. . . ."

I look over at Sammy and see the strangest thing. He has this little smile on his face, and he is slowly shaking his head back and forth as if he can't believe what morons these guys are. Nothing they say or do seems to even bother him, and that makes me smile too.

Sammy voice is big and strong. "Are you ready, Mickey?"

"Ready for what, Dumbo?" Robby and Mitch howl with laughter, like this is the funniest thing they've ever heard.

"Ready for karate, you little creep. Hand-to-hand fighting like we learned right from the Japs. Karate that I learned so I can kick your butt. Haven't you ever heard of karate, you dope?"

Mickey keeps that smirk on his face, but his eyes show another flash of fear. It was just for a second, but I saw it. I think Robby and Mitch saw it too, because they shoot each other a quick look.

"Yeah, karate. Karate that I've studied, and karate that I've taught Josh. Prepare to die, you dopes." And with that, Sammy motions for me to take the fat stick from him and hold it level with the ground just as he had.

With a wink and a smile, Sammy begins a loud chant as he waves his arms in circles and spins around like a ballet dancer. Then without warning, his right hand comes slicing down on the fattest part of the branch, breaking it right in two.

We all stand in stunned silence for a moment until Robby lets out an awed, "Whoa!"

Through locked teeth, I whisper, "How did you do that, Sammy?"

He whispers back, "Easy. I just took two fat sticks and put them together with masking tape and painted it brown back in the Arts and Crafts tent."

I smile and shake my head.

Then he whispers, "Just do everything that I do. You and I are the Bears, okay? We're kicking off to the Lions to start the game. Get it?"

There we are, the two of us with our arms up in the air and our legs in an idiotic dance. Then I hear Sammy howl again, just like he had before he "broke" the branch. He sounds like a deranged animal. I think about my dad's rabbit's foot down in my pocket, protecting me, and then I join Sammy in the loudest, dumbest howl I can imagine. Sammy's voice gets even louder and higher, and he begins to charge right at our three enemies, with his arms flailing over his head.

Okay, why the heck not? We can fool these dopes together. I am only a step behind him, charging right along and without a clue what will happen next.

I guess that Mickey and his jerks don't know what is happening either because just as we get a few feet away, first Mickey, and then the others, turn and begin to run. *Run!* They are running away from us!

We chase them over a ridge and down a hill. We run and we shout and we chase them through another stand of trees and into a small clearing.

I begin to wonder what will happen if we ever catch up with them, but that never happens. What does happen is something I will never forget.

Mickey's escape comes to an abrupt halt when he runs directly into the arms of his uncle, Chief Wellstone, who has just come onto the trail. There are half a dozen other men with him too.

Time seems to stand still, and for a moment, none of this makes any sense. What is Chief Wellstone doing up here on our school trip? And why are our teachers with him?

Mickey has grown suddenly pale and started shaking a little. The chief's cheeks are all wet. Even though his eyes are covered with shiny sunglasses, it's obvious he's been crying. All I can think about is that I don't think I've ever seen a man crying before.

The chief slowly bends down and puts his arm around Mickey, moving him away from the rest of us.

"Josh?"

Just a whisper, but I know the voice right off.

"Josh, we need to talk."

I look behind me and see Al stepping forward from behind some other adults who had also come up the hill. I pull the rabbit's foot out of my pocket and clutch it in both hands. It's pretty cold out, and I wonder why Al is holding his hat in his hands.

I look right up into his sad eyes.

Why are all these people so upset? Why are all these grown men crying?

22

Three Hours before Sarah's Death

I don't know if it's cold in this waiting room, or I'm just scared. Looking over at Sherry sleeping in the chair across from me with her knees drawn up and a blanket covering her shoulders, I guess it's both. I don't realize how cramped up and achy I've become sitting in the same chair for eight hours until I try to get up when I see Dr. Bowman coming out of the operating area. He is beginning the long walk down the hallway to speak with us. I try to read his face, but he is still too far away.

When I first arrived at the National Institutes of Health, it was just after 5:30 p.m. The last time I had driven that fast was to get Sarah to Holy Cross for Sophie's high noon birth. When I heard Dr. Bowman tell me that Sarah's file had come in weeks ago from a Dr. Robert Saber, my world went into hyper speed. It started with a quick call to Sherry to get the kids over to friends so she could meet me, and a mad dash through the first wave of rush hour in D.C.

According to Dr. Bowman, Dr. Saber identified Sarah as the perfect candidate for Level Three. Sadly, this is because she is suffering from what is likely an inoperable pineal tumor. Without the benefit of Level Three, and images from the center of the brain that could for the first time be seen from any angle, Sarah's condition would be considered unsafe for surgery. That would have left only the option to radiate it, and no one expected that to change a sure death sentence.

Dr. Saber had also noted that Sarah's vision was now frequently becoming blurry, particularly when she tried to see things up close, and this indicated that time was of the essence.

When I got Sarah to the National Institutes of Health entrance on Old Georgetown Road, the escort was waiting by the security gate as promised. Good thing, too, because I never would have found this building stuck deep within the enormous science and medical campus.

When our escort stopped directly in front of an unmarked building, Dr. Bowman himself met us at the door and had his attendants carry Sarah out of our car. She was still passed out and needed to be moved onto a gurney.

I was signing the medical release papers in Dr. Bowman's office when they told me that Sherry had arrived. I knew that I didn't have the energy to explain any of this to Sherry, but when she came into the room crying and threw her arms around my neck, I realized that she was only there to help. Maybe for the first time ever, our eyes truly met, and we actually smiled at each other.

Dr. Bowman explained to us both that we were in a very private facility where the NIH did its most experimental testing, typically under a cloak of secrecy. He went on to say that nothing was more secret than his own work on the Level Three Intervention, which is why he was somewhat surprised when his boss gave him a letter from a physician he didn't know named Dr. Saber.

He also said that Dr. Saber seemed to know all about his work and the rare type of patient that was needed to further the testing. The NIH was engaged in research all over the world, and Dr. Bowman's boss made it very clear that whoever Dr. Saber was, he was very well connected.

As I knew from my research at Grand National Insurance, Level Three referred to the new depths of surgery that this technology made possible, surgery that for the first time allowed these scientists to go right to the core of the human brain.

According to Dr. Bowman, Sarah now had only hours, perhaps minutes, to live before the pineal tumor, or what he called a virtual biochemical bomb, ended her life in a flash. I was told that their experimental techniques in magnetic resonance would allow them to see 3-D images of a living brain, the kind of images few had ever seen before, and then be guided to the exact area where the tumor was growing. I was also told, though, that the procedure they were about to attempt had been tried on six previous occasions, and sadly, not a single patient had survived the surgery.

I looked down at the ground when he said that the unwillingness of insurance companies to pay any expenses associated with experimental treatments like Level Three at various research hospitals had further slowed their progress.

But now, in the still of the night, I try to stir my achy body. The hallway from the operating room to where we are sitting seems to stretch out forever. I am still straining to see Dr. Bowman's face as he comes nearer.

He'd make a pretty good poker player. I have no idea what he is about to say. As he approaches, I feel Sherry cling to my side.

"Let's sit down over here and talk. You need to know what's been going on."

I return to my now familiar space in the waiting room, and Dr. Bowman takes the chair by my side.

"Our Level Three images have confirmed exactly what Dr. Saber predicted. Sarah has a classic pineal tumor, whose growth accounts for her painful and frequent headaches. We have isolated the area that needs treatment, and we will be putting her into a medically induced coma so that all her bodily functions will be suspended. At that point, we will attempt to relieve the pressure and, hopefully, remove the tumor from her brain."

It took a moment for me to feel the pain in my arm where Sherry unknowingly dug her nails in.

"Josh, you need to know that this next phase of the surgery is the most critical. And I need to remind you that we have never successfully revived any of the previous patients."

"Do I have a choice here, doc?"

"No. As I told you before, Sarah has only one chance here, and this is it."

I feel another squeeze on my arm, and I look down to see Sherry smiling up at me through her tears.

I turn back to Dr. Bowman. I know that I must sound pitiful as my voice cracks, but I don't care. "Please, doctor, please. Save my Sarah. Do what you need to do."

Dr. Bowman nods and slowly stands up. "Josh, Sherry, we will do all we can on our end. Throw in your very best prayers, and we'll see what happens."

He smiles, turns, and walks briskly back to the operating room. That's when I notice the rabbit's foot clipped to the back of his scrubs. I close my eyes and try to pray, for the first time in years I try to pray, but it's funny—all I can think about is Robert.

23

Two Days after My Father Died

I know people will ask me why I ran out into the rain and snow without even wearing a coat, and all I can think to tell them is that I was hot. I *am* hot, but even more, I just had to get out and away from all those crying, clingy people. Oh yeah, and one more thing: the house stinks.

Some ladies from the neighborhood brought over a bunch of food to feed all the people who had come back to my house from the cemetery. As far as I can tell, and *smell*, most of the food is tuna noodle casserole in these enormous glass bowls that my mom calls Pyrex. Apparently, Pyrex is some kind of miracle because it can go right from the freezer, to the oven, to the refrigerator. Imagine that.

Well, I'll tell you what would be a *real* miracle: getting that house to stop stinking of tuna. But that would be too much to ask for.

I didn't want to run out into the rain. I mean, I'm not crazy, but it was all just more than I could take. Even after Mom let me take my suit jacket off, I still had to keep wearing that stupid tie, and I could feel the tight collar of my only white shirt cutting into my neck.

Earlier, I'd figured the best place to hide out was at the

top of the staircase, so I could watch them all but still be mostly out of sight. Then whenever somebody spotted me and wanted to talk, I could quickly stand up, pretend like I was crying, and run up to my room. But if any of them got a close look at me, I was sure they would have seen that I wasn't even good at *pretending* to cry. So I moved from the stairs to my room, and I sat on my bed for an hour with my closet door open, so I could see myself in the mirror, and I tried and tried to make myself cry.

Come on! What's wrong with you? Are you crazy? Your father just died and you can't even cry.

Off and on, I talked to a few guests who cornered me. There was Tony and Ruthie from Giovanni's. Tony just kept telling me that I was the man of the house now and how my mom was going to need me. Ruthie said, well, to tell you the truth, I don't remember what Ruthie said, but I do remember that crushing hug she gave me sitting next to me on my bed. Ruthie and those beautiful breasts of hers. Okay, she is probably forty, and I am just ten, but she sure is my first love.

The mayor caught me when I was sitting on the steps. He shook my hand like I was an adult and told me that someday I would understand just what a great man my dad was, and how one person can make such a difference in a community. Then he went down the steps and hugged my mom good-bye. He explained that he had to go over to the Wellstones', who lived just a few blocks away. Mickey's dad had been buried a few hours earlier as well.

I guess Al and James must have worked it out so that first one would come up to see me and then the other. Al gave me his "It's okay to cry" speech, which he must have gotten from my mom. And just to show me that he wasn't kidding, he didn't even try to hide his own tears as he spoke.

"Josh, this is the worst day of our lives. You lost your dad, and I lost my best friend."

I just nodded. Wasn't he embarrassed to be crying?

"I know that your dad was always happy that you had such a good friend in Sammy. He would talk about the two of you and how important true friendship is. Keep him close to you, Josh. Keep your friends close. Keep your friends close."

Jeez, he was practically blubbering now. I wonder what he would've said if he'd seen me when we first got back to the house, and Sammy had tried to give me a big hug. Best friend? I'd pulled Sammy's arms off me and told him to go away. I told him that he should just get out, that I never wanted to see him again.

I have decided to blame Sammy for my dad's death. I guess it would have made more sense to blame Mickey's dad. I mean he did shoot my dad. Or even to blame Al, who started all this trouble. But it was *my* dad who got himself killed, so I can blame anyone I want to, and I blame Sammy because his stupid sister was right in the middle of the whole thing. Besides, I just didn't need any friends. I didn't care what anybody said. I didn't need friends, and I didn't even need my dad. All they did was hurt you. All they did was die.

The last person I remember talking to was James. No sooner had Al walked out of my room than James had come in. They met up in the doorway and just stood there for a few seconds, not saying a word. But I'm not stupid, and I know they were both thinking about what to do with me. I was surprised to see Al put his hand on James's shoulder and then slowly move on.

James took Al's spot on the bed next to me. "Josh, how about coming downstairs now? Most of the people are starting to leave, and I think it would be a good time to go and sit with your mom."

"My mom?" I'd kind of forgotten about her.

"Josh, your mom is going to really need you."

"I'll go down and help clean up later, okay? Right now, I just want to be alone."

"No, I don't mean she needs your help like that. I just mean that now that your dad is gone, your mom is going to really need your help."

I just looked up at him and tried to understand what he was saying.

"You know that I was just about your age when I lost my father too. Did you know that?"

"Sure, James. I know all about you. I know your father drove a bus, and some crazy man shot him when you were a kid like me. I know that you had four little brothers and sisters and that you were only twelve when my dad hired you to do some errands around his store after school every day. I know that he helped you go to college at night after working for him during the day. I know that you enlisted when the war in Korea started, and I know that they sent you to Officer's School after you scored third out of 15,000 soldiers who took the test. I know that you got some medals, and I know everything there is to know about you."

I don't know why, but the more I spoke, the more I started to get mad at James too. I'd known James my whole life, and I'd never been mad at him before, but now I couldn't help it. Especially as he started smiling halfway through my showing him that I knew all about him.

Then he said, "Well, I'll tell you something about me that you don't know. You don't know that half the time, your dad would call me 'Josh.' Did you know that? Did you know that he'd call me by your name?"

I didn't want to hear this right now, and I punched the pillow with the back of my fist. I spoke through gritted teeth. "And he called me James. Not on purpose, I know, but sometimes I thought he was doing it just to make me mad at him. But he'd laugh and say 'sorry,' and I knew that he wasn't kidding about it being an accident. But one day when he called me James, I yelled at him, 'I'm your *son*, I'm Josh. Quit calling me James!' Even then, he just laughed and gave me a hug. Then he looked me right in the eye and smiled and said, I'm sorry, it's just that I love you both the same."

I looked over to James, who slowly got to his feet. He looked so sad, and all I could think was, *Don't you start crying too!* "Go on down to your mom now, Josh. Go on now." And with that he turned and slowly walked out of my room.

I sat alone for a little while longer, and then I saw it over on my desk: that stupid rabbit's foot just sitting there, like it was looking back at me and laughing. What a joke! Lucky, huh? I don't need that kind of luck.

I grabbed the rabbit's foot and stuck it deep into my pocket, then flew down the steps and out the front door before anybody else had a chance to get me alone to tell me what a great person my dad was.

I don't even remember running through the slushy snow, but now that I've stopped, I can feel the cold water running over my feet. Now I'm standing right by the curb, the gutter, where the melting snow has turned into a little river. Over and around my now soaked feet, it races a few feet farther down to the open grate of the sewer.

So here I am, a ten-year-old man, standing on the street curb in the cold, blowy Indiana rain, looking down at my soaking feet, now almost ankle-deep in a miniature river racing down to the drain a few feet away. Thrusting my freezing hands deep down into my pockets I feel it, soft and fluffy on the outside, hard bone on the inside. And I know right then what I am going to do.

I yank it out of my pocket and throw it into the little river at my feet. Then I stand there, watching with grim satisfaction as the water carries it away toward the drain, slowly at first and then faster. But then, as if to mock me, it just floats there, right over the steel slats of the street drain, just bobbing up and down, caught somehow, I suppose. It seems to be asking me, "Are you sure, Josh? Are you really sure?" But I just stand there in the rain, not wanting a second chance, just watching, watching, watching, and then in a flash, it's gone.

Down the drain. Into the dark. See you later, Dad.

24

When Sarah Dies

D r. Bowman later told me a team of nine top surgeons and surgical nurses worked together in a carefully orchestrated step-by-step plan to go deeper and deeper to the core of Sarah's brain.

He said that on all six previous attempts to remove a pineal tumor, he had tried to find the right path to the very center of the brain—what he said was literally referred to as the "seat of the soul"—before one wrong turn led to intracerebral hemorrhaging and a quick death.

What he didn't tell me, what even he didn't know, and what none of them could see, was that even with her eyes closed, Sarah looked up from the surgical table when she heard a familiar voice calling her with a friendly, soothing, "Hello, Sarah."

To Sarah, it was as if she were awakening from a deep, restful sleep, and it seemed perfectly natural to her to see a smiling Robert standing in between all the doctors and nurses gazing down on her. It didn't even seem strange that while everyone else was wearing surgical scrubs, Robert was nattily dressed in golf attire, right down to the putter in his hand.

"It's nice to see you again, Sarah. How are you feeling?"

Sarah thought for a moment. Something seemed different, but at first she couldn't place it. And then she knew. It was her head. For the first time in as long as she could remember, it didn't hurt.

"Better, Robert. I feel *much* better!"

A moment later though, Sarah heard a sharp alarm coming from behind the others.

Curious now, she asked Robert what all the commotion was about. It didn't seem the least bit strange to her that no one in the room even noticed Robert or the conversation they were enjoying.

"Well, it looks like you are giving these fine doctors a very tough time of it."

Sarah could hear the alarms, and she could sense the tension in the medical team's voices, but she didn't feel afraid, not even when she heard one of the nurses, who was standing next to the blaring monitor, say, "We're losing her, doctor. She's crashing!"

"Robert, I can't see what they're doing."

"Come over here. We'll have a much better view."

And it didn't even seem strange to Sarah that she and Robert were floating up by the high ceiling so they could look down on Sarah's body and have the perfect view of the whole scene. They saw the monitor, which now showed a constant flat line, and they saw the nurses and doctors switching from a failed attempt at CPR to applying electric paddles to her chest. She could see that her body was convulsing with each shock, but a quick glance over to the monitor showed that it was in vain.

They looked down at Dr. Bowman, who stood transfixed over her body. "Turn that damn thing off."

"Are you calling it, doctor?"

Dr. Bowman tugged off his surgical mask. He looked so sad as he turned to his colleagues. "I really thought she'd make it. Each time we go in, we solve another piece of the puzzle and now . . . now we know."

And then she saw one of the other doctors, a young woman, put her hand on his shoulder. "Dr. Bowman, you are to be congratulated. You've done it. You've found the path to the core, the very seat of the soul. This is a magnificent night for us all."

Dr. Bowman smiled weakly.

"Not for us all, Dr. Yang. Time of death: 5:01 a.m."

Sarah turned back to Robert. "Am I dead now?"

"I don't know. They don't tell me everything. What do you think about dying? You were in an awful lot of pain. Remember?"

Sarah thought for a moment, and then in the calmest of voices, she told him, "No, Robert. I think it's better if I don't die just yet. Josh still needs me, and so do the kids."

Robert smiled warmly. "Then you better get back down there and make a fight of it. Those nice doctors look like they have given up on you."

"Is that why you came to us? Did you come here to save my life?"

"No, Sarah. I'm sorry, but I didn't come to save you. I came to save Josh."

Sarah nodded. She knew exactly what he meant, and she knew, too, exactly what to do.

"Thank you, Robert." Sarah bent forward to kiss his cheek, but in an instant, Robert was gone, and Sarah was quickly moving back inside herself.

But then everything, everything went black.

———————

I stood there, watching with grim satisfaction as the water carried the rabbit's foot toward the drain, slowly at first and then faster. But then, as if to mock me, it just floated there, right over the steel slats of the street drain, just bobbing up and down, caught somehow. It seemed to be asking me, "Are you sure, Josh? Are you really sure?" But I just stood there in the rain, not wanting a second chance, just watching, watching, watching, and then, then I looked up to see an enormous black sedan turning onto my street. Not a common sight in Hammond, Indiana. Except for in the movies, I'd never seen anything like it.

I watched as the car pulled to a stop right across the street from where I was standing in the gutter. For a moment, the car just sat there, and I couldn't see anything through the windows, but then the back door opened, and a man stepped out. He was wearing a dark suit and sunglasses, and he slowly walked over until he stood right in front of me.

"Josh Brown?"

"Yes sir."

"I am special agent Spalding with the United Nation's World Crisis Agency." He took out his badge and flipped it open, but it gleamed in the sun, and I really couldn't read anything before, in a single motion, he flipped it closed and smoothly slid it back into his breast pocket.

"May I have a word with you in private, please?" Agent

Spalding motioned to the car, where a driver, also in a dark suit, was now standing next to an open rear door. Without hesitation, I walked over to the car and climbed into the backseat. Agent Spalding silently joined me.

"What I'm going to tell you now must never be repeated. Do you understand?" I knew that even trying to speak would be fruitless, so I just nodded.

"I am under direct orders from the President of the United States, the Queen of England, and other governments around the world to share with you that your father is still alive. His death was staged, and he is deep, deep undercover on a mission vital to the future of our planet. Do you understand?"

I knew it! I knew he was alive! I nodded again that I understood, but I was now able to ask in a whisper, "Can I see him?"

"No, you can't see him, and you may never be able to. You can't even tell your mother about this, and that comes right from the White House, young man. It's just that your father loves you very much, and he was given special consideration, because of how much he has sacrificed, to let you know that he is alive, he is out there, and he is very proud of you. Josh, your father is a great man. A brave man. A man the whole world is counting on."

Once more I nodded. I tried to talk. I tried to tell Agent Spalding that I understood, but I couldn't speak. I tried to tell him that this secret, this secret of worldwide security, was safe with me, safe with this hero's son, but I couldn't make the words come out. I still couldn't see Agent Spalding's eyes through the sunglasses, and I suddenly felt a wave of panic. Why can't I talk?

And then I felt a strong hand gripping my shoulder. I felt the hand shaking me harder and harder. Had someone else gotten into the car? Who was shaking me? It was Agent Spalding's driver, but why? I reached up and slowly pulled off the driver's sunglasses, and I looked into his face, that face, I know that face, but it doesn't make sense. Why is Dr. Bowman here?

———————

"Wake up, Josh. Wake up. You're having a nightmare."

And then slowly I wake up. I wake up from the same dream I've had every night since my father died.

"Wake up. We need to speak."

I try to stir my body from the waiting room chair. I look deep into Dr. Bowman's eyes. I know that I am still half asleep. I know too that I don't want to hear what he is about to tell me.

25

Three Days after My Father Died

My mom told me that the morning after we buried my dad, James and Al met at eight a.m. over at Lucky Auto to open up. Mom said that was the day their friendship began.

They never spoke about it. They never said anything dopey like Sammy would say: *Gee, Josh, you're my best friend. You know that, Josh, we're best friends.* I mean that was fine to say when we were in the first or second grade, but I'm ten years old now, and guys don't talk like that.

Al and James didn't have to talk about being friends. It just happened. And they didn't have to tell each other. They just were.

When lunchtime came that first day, they both knew where they'd be going. Just before noon, they went into the bathroom and changed clothes. They both put on their old army uniforms, medals and all, just as they'd planned over at my house the day before. My mom said she heard that James looked very fit and handsome, but she laughed when she told me that James had to help Al button his army jacket, which was almost bursting at the seams.

They got into Al's car and drove right over to the clubhouse at the Northwest Park Public Golf Course, a

201

year-round hangout for some locals, even when the course itself is under a foot of snow. I'm told they didn't talk too much on the way over, but as they were about to get out of the car, Al said to James, "Well, Lieutenant. Are you ready?"

James looked over at Al's uniform with its small handful of assorted medals and ribbons.

He pointed. "What's that bronze one? The medal next to the Purple Heart?"

Al looked down at his own chest and smiled broadly. "That's for marksmanship. I earned it when we graduated from boot camp."

"Marksmanship! You shot your best friend, and they'd given you a medal for marksmanship?"

They shared a good laugh as they trudged along the shoveled path leading to the clubhouse. Entering the simple wooden room, they paused briefly at the front door and then just smiled at the largely male crowd seated at the various tables and lunch counter. They slowly made their way over to an open table toward the back of the room and sat right under a sign that said "No Jews or Coloreds Allowed."

And no one said a word, not one word, but there must have been twenty open-mouthed faces staring right at them.

Al pointed up at the sign and looked over to James. "You know, I think we're doing this all wrong."

"Why's that?"

"Well, Lieutenant, you're sitting under the word 'Jews,' and I'm sitting where it says 'Coloreds.' I don't know. It just seems like we've got it all wrong."

The two men shared a good laugh and broadly smiled at the gawkers, all the while pointing at the sign. Then they each stood up and moved around the table, exchanging seats.

As they sat back down, James proclaimed loudly and laughingly to no one in particular, "Now, that's better, isn't it?"

The next day Al and James went back to the Northwest Park clubhouse, and it was the same thing all over again. Except this time, that sign was down.

My mom said it was their last gift to my dad. She said he would have been pleased.

———

About the same time Al and James were having lunch, I was home, in my room, where I'd gone well before the last of the guests had left our house the night before. I was thinking about how my life would go if I never left it again. Last night, I'd even tried not to go to sleep. I was afraid to go to sleep, actually—afraid of ghosts in this house of death—but finally I did drift off, and dreamed of a special agent Spalding.

Mom knocks on my door.

"It's nearly noon, buddy. You have to get up now."

"Go away."

"Come on down. I'm making you a grilled cheese, bacon too, if you'd like."

"Not hungry."

"Josh, come on down. You've got a guest here to see you."

Can it be? Can it be Agent Spalding? "Is it a man wearing sunglasses?"

"What? Don't be silly. It's Sammy, for God's sake. Sammy's downstairs, and he wants to be with you. He got all the kids in your class to write you letters, and he wants you to have them. Now, don't be rude. Come on down."

Well, I haven't eaten in a couple of days, and my stomach hurts from being empty. "Okay, I'm coming."

I slowly walk from my room to the top of the steps and look down to the front door. Just last week I stood in this exact spot and watched as my dad ran out into the winter cold to get Al out of jail. It has only been a few days, but it seems so long ago now.

In the kitchen, Sammy has his face buried in a bowl of Campbell's Tomato Soup, his free hand like a claw around a grilled cheese sandwich. Not a pretty picture, and it only gets worse when Sammy looks up and gives me an enormous smile with a mouth full of soup and sandwich. Ugh.

"What are you grinning at?" I decide I am entitled to feel sorry for myself right now. "Don't you remember that my father just died?"

I see a little of flash of pain in Sammy's eyes. "I remember. It's just that I smile whenever I see you. You're my best friend."

"Yeah, I know. I know because you tell me that every five minutes."

Sammy hesitates for just a moment. "Oh, I almost forgot. Look what I have for you." He pulls out a big brown folder held shut by a heavy string. "It's from all the kids. They all wanted to write something to you to make you feel better."

Sammy slides the folder across the table to me.

"How did they do this? There hasn't been any school since my dad died."

"Oh, well, I guess I helped a little. On Saturday your mom said you were too upset to see anybody, so I went to each of the kids' houses from our class and I asked them to do it. Then I went back yesterday to pick them up."

I didn't want him doing any of this. "You did what?"

"Yeah. I just told them it was for my best friend, and they all said okay. So here you go." And with that he pushes the folder closer.

He just doesn't get it. With the back of my hand, I push the folder off the table so hard that when it hits the floor, it comes open and the papers go flying all over the kitchen just as I fly out of my seat.

"Go away, Sammy! I don't want you here anymore, and I don't want you telling everybody that we're best friends anymore, because we aren't."

I want to keep screaming at him. If I scream enough, he might start crying. Crying like a baby. I haven't cried, not once. Not even when I tried to make myself cry last night. So maybe if I can't make myself cry, I can make others cry. Why not?

Now Sammy is up from his seat too, and his chubby face is bright red. For the first time ever, Sammy yells at me.

"Why are you being so mean? I'm just trying to help you. And you *are* my best friend. I don't care what you say. Don't you remember up in Wisconsin, when those guys stopped us? We stuck together and we scared them. We scared them, and they started running away. We stood there together, and they were backing down."

"Right. They were really afraid of us. The three toughest kids in the school against the two of us, and they were afraid. They probably would've turned around when we got closer and just creamed us." I do my best to roll my eyes.

"They were running away! They were afraid of us and you know it."

"All I know is that before they could beat the crap out of us again, everyone showed up to tell us Mickey's dad and my dad were both dead. That's what I know."

"Come on, Josh."

Finally, Sammy is starting to cry.

"Get out of here, Sammy. I don't want to be your friend. I don't need you. I don't even need my dad. I don't need anybody."

I mean it. I wouldn't have thrown away my father's stupid rabbit's foot if I still needed him. I've backed Sammy all the way to the front door, which I now hold open against the cold winter wind. With a final push, I have him out the door, dragging his coat behind him. Yeah, he is crying pretty good now. He is crying so hard that when I slam the door shut, I can barely understand him and his blubbering.

But still, I know what he is saying.

"You'll come back to me, Josh. You'll come back."

26

The Day Sarah Dies

D r. Bowman's face has come into focus, but I don't like what I am seeing in his eyes. Sherry has thrown off her blanket, and she looks just as scared as I am.

"Josh. Sherry. We need to talk."

Sherry collapses against me and lets out the most mournful sob I've heard since that day back at my house in Hammond.

Dr. Bowman moves even closer to us both.

"Sarah's not dead, but she's not out of the woods either."

I reply without any satisfaction, "So the Level Three Intervention still doesn't work?"

"Level Three allowed us to have a picture of exactly where the tumor was, deep inside Sarah's brain. With that image, we were able to find a path right to the core, and surgically, we were able to get most of it removed. We relieved a lot of the pressure too, so at least for whatever time she has left, she won't have to suffer through those horrible headaches anymore."

"And how much time is that, doctor?"

"There's no way of knowing. It could be anytime. Days? Months? We do know that if you hadn't brought her in when you did, she wouldn't be alive right now. The mass started to cause hemorrhaging during surgery. There was one point where we'd thought we'd lost her. According to our monitors, her heart, her brain waves, all her vital signs had blanked out. We were about to leave her in peace when she came back to us."

Sherry asks, "You saw the monitors go off, and then you saw them come back on?"

"Yes, but that wasn't how we knew she'd come back to us." Dr. Bowman pauses, as if he's trying to relive the moment just as it happened. "It wasn't the monitors, it was Sarah. One minute she appeared to have passed on. One of the surgical nurses had removed the tube from her mouth, and the next thing we knew, Sarah started talking to us!"

I can't believe what I'm hearing.

"The operating room erupted in excitement, and I had to call for silence, but we heard her. We heard her as clear as a bell."

"What was she saying?"

"She said 'Angela.'"

Sherry slowly shakes her head. "Angela? I don't know an Angela." She pleads for more. "That's it? Just *Angela*?"

"At first she just kept repeating Angela over and over, but before she stopped, she suddenly opened her eyes, looked right at me, and said, 'Tell Josh he must save Angela.' Just like that. Just like we were having a cup of coffee or something. Then she closed her eyes as if to say, Okay, you can finish now. Thirty years of neurosurgery, and I've never seen anything like it!"

Sherry, still in shock, whispers, "But what does it mean?"

"The human brain is a mystery, and we're going places

and doing things with Level Three that have never been done before. I don't know what it means. All I know is that Sarah is alive, but the tumor isn't completely gone, and I'm sorry, but she can die without warning at any time."

Sherry sounds like a little child when she asks, "What can we do?"

"All I can tell you both is to love her with all your heart. Look at each and every day together as a blessing. That's all you can do. That's all any of us can do."

After a moment or two, Sherry and Dr. Bowman both look over at me. I'm just staring off into space. I didn't hear much of what the doctor said, but I did hear him say there wasn't much we could do.

And one more thing. He said "Angela." I heard him say "Angela."

I'm up on my feet. "No. There's plenty we can do!"

"Are you all right?"

I look down at the kind doctor. "I need a driver and an ambulance, Dr. Bowman. And I need you to have your team get ready to scrub in again."

The doctor looks at me like I'm crazy. "And where are you going?"

Sherry smiles and answers for me. "I don't know for sure, doctor, but if I had to guess, I'd say he's going to get somebody named Angela."

———

The beltway traffic is pretty normal for a Tuesday D.C. rush hour, but the ambulance cuts through it at a steady pace, and once we get to Baltimore, the driver knows the best local roads to take us to St. Agnes.

Back at the NIH, Dr. Bowman hadn't hesitated for a moment once I told him where I was off to. I suppose having just seen a miracle in the operating room, he decided he could cut through the red tape. He even got a laugh out of my authorizing the surgery as an officer of Grand National Insurance on behalf of a bona fide policyholder.

Now less than an hour later, the ambulance is pulling up to the emergency room entrance of the aged St. Agnes Hospital in Southwest Baltimore. And thanks to a call from Dr. Bowman, a nurse and a nun are waiting for me by the entrance so they can escort me to a room in pediatric intensive care.

Going down the hall, the nun asks, "Excuse me, but how do you know Mr. Scappelli?"

I answer without breaking stride. "I don't know him, sister. Or his wife either. We've only spoken on the phone."

"There is no Mrs. Scappelli, Mr. Brown. She died during childbirth. Angela is all Mr. Scappelli has, poor soul."

My heart briefly stops, but my feet go even faster. As we approach the closed room's door, the nun blocks my way and gives me an icy stare.

"You know, when I told him you were coming, he asked me, what for? He told me to tell you that you were the last person he'd ever want to see."

I try to speak, but the words don't come easily. "Sister, please . . ."

She doesn't say another word—just stares deeply into my eyes.

"Please, sister."

And with that, she silently opens the door and quickly closes it right behind me.

———

The room is nearly dark except for the soft glow of the monitors next to the little girl's bed. I see a lone figure standing at her side, holding her hand. He speaks without turning to face me.

"It's too late, Mr. Brown. You've come too late. Let's just let her lie here in peace."

The monitor shows that although her heart is beating slowly, little Angela, so tiny in her bed, is still alive.

"Mr. Scappelli, I have an ambulance downstairs and the best doctors back in D.C. They are ready to operate as soon as we arrive. Please, Mr. Scappelli. We have to try."

Anthony Scappelli turns toward me. He has a kind face. Tired and sad, but kind. Then he turns back to look at his little Angela.

"No. No more. Please, just go. Just leave us alone."

I stand there in silence, not knowing what to do, just knowing that I have failed, and this family will suffer because of me. I close my eyes.

"Listen to him, Anthony."

The voice comes from over my shoulder from an even darker corner of the room, but I don't have to turn around to know who it is.

"Anthony, please do as he says. If he tells you that Angela can be saved, then you have to trust him."

Mr. Scappelli answers sadly. "What do you know? You're

not a doctor. You're a lawyer." And then with a sad chuckle he adds, "And maybe not even a good one at that."

I can't move a muscle. When I open my eyes, I see a big brute of a man with his arm around Mr. Scappelli's shoulder.

"Come on. If he says he can do it, then he can do it. Come on, Anthony."

And then Sammy looks up at me and smiles.

"I told you you'd come back."

Epilogue

Sarah's Funeral

Thinking about the weather isn't usually considered strange. Still, here I am, sitting at my own wife's funeral, and sonofabitch, would you believe I'm thinking about the weather.

It seems like only from a distance that I hear the words of those who stand by Sarah's coffin to speak. I can hear some crying, too, especially the pitiful tiny sobs of the small children I love, but none of that is in my mind right now. Just the weather.

It's the sunlight that's throwing me off. Funerals are meant to be held on dark, rainy days. But here I am, sitting in the chapel, and all I can see is the brilliant Maryland winter sunlight *gushing* through the stained-glass windows and shining a spotlight on Sarah's coffin.

I try to focus on the words of the speaker, the last to eulogize my Sarah. It is Richie talking. Richie Jr., actually— Richie and Angela's oldest son, our first grandchild, and the spitting image of his mother. Richie Jr. is talking about what a great woman his grandmother was and how his own children, the ones I hear softly crying, were so blessed to get to know this amazing woman.

But no one has been more blessed than I have been. My years with Sarah saw our love grow beyond anything either of us could have imagined. Knowing that I could lose Sarah at any time made me cherish her all the more. Every glance. Every smile. Every breath.

Dr. Bowman was right that night. He told us that Sarah could die at any time, and she did. She died peacefully in her sleep nearly fifty years after that fateful night, the night that marked the end of four days that changed my life forever. That night also changed the face of modern medicine. In 1986, three years after the experimental surgeries on Sarah and Angela, a FONAR scanner at the UCLA Medical Center became the world's first MRI in which an interventional surgical procedure was performed. Surgery has never been the same since.

Richie Jr. is through talking now. Everyone is starting to gather around me. I'm only eighty-five, for God's sake, but they treat me like I'm fragile. I'm still working too. Sammy passed on last fall, but Brown & Johnson, Attorneys at Law, is still going strong. Still standing together against those bullies.

We start to move together toward the door when I hear his voice. "Hello, Josh."

He looks as handsome as ever. He is wearing the same beautiful suit he had on when I saw him that night in the casino.

"Hello, Robert. I had a hunch you'd be here today."

"I loved Sarah. I wouldn't have missed it for the world."

"You look the same. Fifty years now, but you look the same."

Robert flashes that smile, and we embrace. His touch warms me to the soul. "I'm proud of you, Josh. No father could ever be prouder."

"Thank you. Thank you fifty times over for what you've given me."

We stand at arm's length now, and I am oblivious to the crowd gathered round. Somehow I'm not surprised that no one is paying the least bit of attention to Robert. At first I think I am the only one who can even see him, but then I feel a persistent tug on my pants leg. I look down at little Matthew, five years old, our first great-grandchild.

"Who's that, Poppy? Who is that man?"

Robert bends down and puts Matthew's hands in his.

"I'm his old golfing buddy, son. We go way back."

Then Robert whispers something in Matthew's ear before he stands back up and my family starts to move me away.

"When are we going to get another golf game in?" I ask him. "Or maybe catch a football game on the tube? I'm getting pretty tired these days."

Robert starts to disappear as even more people come between us, but his words carry clearly back to me.

"Soon, Josh. Very soon."

―――――――

Josh is now completely surrounded by those he loves and those who love him. They all know that the day will come when he too will be leaving them.

Everyone is focused on Josh except the little boy at his side, who opens his hand to see what the nice man has just given him. It's all burned and dented, but the man had whispered in his ear that it was very old and meant for good luck. But still he wondered, was it really a rabbit's foot?

THE END

A Message from the Author

Creating Rabbit's Foot has been a labor of love for me, and now that you've read it, I would love to hear from you. I can be reached on Facebook by searching *Rabbit's Foot A Gift from My Father* where you can click on an image of the book's cover. You can also post questions on our web site, www.rabbitsfootbook.com or by writing to me at Allan@ rabbitsfootbook.com.

I also ask that if you enjoyed the book, and especially if you feel that this story is really a message that is worth sharing, please reach out to your friends and help spread the word. You can also post your comments and questions on the *Rabbit's Foot* page as well, and if you are a true fan, please take a moment to post a review on www.amazon.com and other online book discussions.

In the coming weeks you may see other features on our Facebook page, including interviews, Q&As, and even the opportunity to learn about a virtual book club.

Thank you for reading my book. Now put it down and start telling your friends!

Allan Horlick

Acknowledgments

This book has been a labor of love for many years, and I have drawn upon the help and guidance of some extremely talented people. I'm thankful for the guidance that I received in the earliest phase of this process from Ken Atchity and the early-on editing of Dawn Grey. Later, as the book started to become a reality, I'm particularly grateful for the advice given to me by Jeff Kleinman of Folio, and the leadership shown by my ultimate publishing "go-to" guy, Mike Vezo.

Mike not only gave me the benefit of his own substantial experience, but he also established the connection for me to several very talented women: artist Bonnie Counts-Bright and line editors Kirsteen Anderson and Melanie Mallon.

Rabbit's Foot is a story about the positive power of relationships, and in that area I have been uniquely fortunate. I have many people to thank for their friendship and support, too many to list, but allow me to name a few. First off, there is real power that comes from making new friends. They can broaden you, teach you, and inspire you. Three new friends that fit that bill for me are Sam Horn, Dr. Nisha Money, and Willie Jolley. But don't take my word for it, you can Google them and see for yourself. Willie introduced me to Sam, who introduced me to Nisha as well as Mike Vezo. It is truly amazing to see how much positive power these folks can generate.

And then there are some old friends, starting with some longtime broadcasting buddies. Going back to my early broadcasting days there's Dick Lobo, Dick Reingold, Jim Corboy, Pat Wallace, and a remarkable couple, Mike and Maureen Ward. With the exception of Maureen (who is the smartest one of this group), we all met in Chicago many years ago, where that part of my journey began.

In my early and confusing "adult" days, as I was trying to find the best way forward, I was fortunate to have my friendships with now Illinois State Representative Sid Mathias and his wife, Rita, along with an old college buddy, Jeff Krause, and his wife, Bonnie. Looking back on it, there's no question that we all helped each other to grow up.

I'd be remiss if I didn't acknowledge Drs. Bruce and Sandra Garrett, great friends over the years, and Jeff Klein, who always takes my family's matters to heart. In *Rabbit's Foot*, Josh is blessed to have a great friend named Sammy. For me, Sammy is longtime friend Rob Ades. Rob is the original "he'll pick you up at 3am when your car breaks down" kind of guy. I've lost track of all the kindnesses he has shown me over the years, but in the pluses and minuses of life, I am deeply indebted to him.

While this book is dedicated to the memory of my father, I want you to know that my late mother was also a remarkable person. She was smart, funny, and loyal—not a bad trifecta, and she is deeply missed.

We all need someone to be proud of, and I have two: my children, Neil and Ellen. It boggles my mind to think about how many lives each of them has already touched, and they have both only just begun.

Saving the best for last is an easy call for me…..my wife, Darlene. As of this writing, we have shared nearly four decades of love and friendship. I wouldn't know where to begin in telling you how lucky I am, but beyond the fact that she is beautiful, she also turned out to be a great editor. Dar was the first person to read and edit every chapter of this book, and she was there for me every step of the way. But then, she always has been. I've dragged Dar around the world and sometimes from one crazy scheme to another, but she's never left my side. If I wake up tomorrow and tell her that I've decided to become a cowboy, or an astronaut, or a shepherd, she'd be fine with that too. Just as long as we're together.

Reader's Club Discussion Guide

Discussion topics

1. The central theme behind *Rabbit's Foot* is to appreciate every moment of your life and especially the people you love. Was this easier to do in 1959 and even 1983 than it is today?

2. Sammy and Josh were both victims of school bullying, which is very much a part of today's headlines. Was it different when we were kids? Adults can be bullied as well. Was Anthony Scappelli's treatment from Grand National a form of bullying?

3. There is a special bond between a son and his father, and much has been written and discussed about the need for a positive male role model in a young boy's life. After Bob died, do you think that in his absence, Josh forgot the life lessons he had been taught, or that he chose to reject them out of anger for life being so unfair to him?

4. Many people believe that few blessings are as dear as lifelong friendships. As you grow older and grow apart, do you need to have a temporary "break-up" before you really appreciate your old friends?

5. Do you believe in good luck? Is there power in a talisman like a rabbit's foot by simply thinking there is?

6. When you are young and you lose someone you love, does it make you less open to trusting and unconditionally giving your heart to someone else? If so, how do you get beyond this?

7. At any point in your life, when you lose someone you love, can it make you reject their values and what they stood for, perhaps to punish them for leaving you?

8. Who do you think Robert was? In his letter to Josh, he said the question wasn't whether his late father came back to him, but rather that he had never left him. Maybe we just need to do a better job of remembering?

9. Can being a loyal fan of a sports team go too far, or is it a healthy distraction from the pressures of everyday life?

10. Does it take more courage to stand up for your friend in a small town where everyone knows each other, or in a big city where people may be busier and more cynical?

A Conversation with Allan Horlick

Question: Why did you write *Rabbit's Foot*?
Answer: I wanted to make people happy and inspire them to appreciate their lives and their loved ones. We are living through a very stressful period in history, and we are coming to realize that it is more important than ever for us to focus on what is really important in life, and that starts with the people that we love.

Question: How did you enjoy the writing process?
Answer: My favorite part was that I loved hanging out with the characters. I'm pretty straight, and growing up I was never into drugs in a big way, so it was kind of mystical for me to find that after a few minutes of writing, I was actually taking a trip back in time where I could be with some people of my own invention that I really liked hanging out with.

Question: Why did you tell this story as a book and not a movie?
Answer: I actually wanted to write a movie, and I saw every chapter in my head as a scene from a movie. A book seemed to me an easier way to get the story out there for people to enjoy, but I hope that it does become a movie someday. I've had many conversations with my family and friends where we play the game of speculating which actors and actresses we would want to cast for each role. The best debate always centers on whether one actor could play Bob as a soldier in 1945, a father in 1959, and an older man in 1983? Let's find out who did Brad Pitt's makeup in Benjamin Button!

Question: What books, movies, and plays inspired you to write *Rabbit's Foot*?

Answer: There are two movies that I love for the feelings they bring out in me. The first is Albert Brooks' *Defending Your Life*, and the other is *Field of Dreams*. My favorite play is Thornton Wilder's *Our Town*. There are too many books to list, but I love the way Charles Frazier told the story *Cold Mountain*, and in particular how every chapter brought the two main characters closer together as it followed their individual trials and adventures.

I would love to hear from any of my readers with questions of your own, which you can send to our website at www.rabbitsfootbook.com or on Facebook at Rabbit's Foot A Gift from My Father book.

Allan Horlick